THE CRYSTAL CLEAR CASE

BY LEE HEAD

THE FIRST OF JANUARY
THE TERRARIUM

The Crystal Clear Case

LEE HEAD

G.P. PUTNAM'S SONS, NEW YORK

SBN: 399-11984-1

Library of Congress Cataloging in Publication Data

Head, Lee.
   The crystal clear case.

   I. Title
PZ4.H4332Cr [PS3558.E15] 813'.5'4 77-8431

 Printed in the United States of America

"Every calculation based on expectations elsewhere, fails in New Mexico."

LEW WALLACE
Territorial Governor
(sign in El Patio bar, Taos, New Mexico)

THE CRYSTAL CLEAR CASE

Chapter One

By five P.M. on Monday, March 1, Lexey Jane Pelazoni felt as if someone had slammed all of her in a door. "I'm a sentimental old fool," she thought angrily, "to do this when I could have flown."

But it had been such an unexpected chance. From the moment she stepped into Julien Strauss' office and he told her of his discovery, she had begun to form the plan.

"I want you to see this before I call Mrs. Mueller," he'd told her.

"No, no. Don't call her, Julien." She smiled benignly at her portfolio manager. "She's not well, and news like this could . . . well, it could kill her." She rested a hand on her cane with an air of finality.

Julien narrowed his eyes at the frail old lady. "She's as healthy as a horse and you know it. But you're not." He pointed a finger at her.

"Oh, but I'm telling the truth, Julien. Her asthma, you

know," and Lexey Jane had placed a soulful gloved hand against the bosom of her Saint Laurent jacket.

"The last time you went flying around the country, you almost got killed."

"I'm not flying, Julien. I'm taking the train."

"The train!" Julien spluttered, his jowls trembling.

"I am going, Julien." She tossed her gray head defiantly, already remembering the huge snorting, charging locomotives of her youth—the cradle-rocking tranquility, the time to think. A journey back into history. That pleased her, even if her errand was most unpleasant. And, as always now, she felt time pressing against her, the world changing with jetlike speed. She had actually bristled that day in Julien's office. Somebody was stealing all her trains. And if she didn't hurry, they would steal this one too. The Santa Fe Chief, that grand old chin-thrust-forward remnant of the Atchison-Topeka-and Santa Fe. The great train line that had crisscrossed the midwest with the throb of Judy Garland's voice in its wheels.

But she'd forgotten that her bones were younger then. Now, after days and nights of tossing, they were sore to the marrow, pained even more by the letter she'd received just before leaving. Inches away on the seat she saw the corner of the envelope sticking from her purse. She reached for it and read it once more, a hastily scrawled note from Rebecca West.

"I sadly report they are tearing down our lovely little home in Ibstone to make room for a ghastly apartment complex. It seems that all the good and beautiful things in life must go," the voice wailed to her from across the Atlantic.

Lexey Jane leaned back and closed her eyes. She could see the rock wall and garden, the steps that rose up to the front door. Those steps. How she and the nurse had laughed when they carried the pram down them. Her bones had not hurt then. And Anne was still alive. "Ambassador Bingham called me today," Augustus had told her somewhere far back in her youth. "He wants me to assist him at St. Jame's."

"We're going to England!" she had cried, flinging her arms around her husband's neck. And with that same joyous excitement they had moved into the house in Ibstone and begun Anne.

The train bolted around a curve, throwing her sideways. The letter popped from her lap and fluttered to the floor of the compartment. She opened her eyes and glared at the sheet of folded paper.

In another garden it had all ended. The day was indelible in her memory. Even with age, that one moment refused to fade, like those ancient dyes on the caves in France, still vivid with color. Anne was coming home from Europe with her new husband. Lexey Jane had stepped into the garden in Wilmington with the shears. It was November. She was forty years old. Chrysanthemums were in bloom. The air was cool, the sun hot on her back. She was wearing a navy blue crepe piped in white around the neck, and she had bent over to snip off a golden mum. The pain pierced her spine like a long spike. She dropped to her knees, hunched over, thinking, "I'll soil my dress." Sparks of white light shot in front of her eyes. "It will go away in a minute." She could feel the crepe sticking to her skin, little beads of perspiration form along her upper lip and beneath the clipped bangs on her forehead. After thirty minutes, she began crawling on her hands and knees toward the kitchen door.

Pain.

Anne came home with her German husband, a swarthy

brute covered with hair, who roamed the big house in his undershirt and trousers. Lexey Jane loathed and distrusted him. And then Anne's mysterious death. "An aneurysm," the doctor told her.

"She was murdered," she had cried back. "He did it! I know he did it." The German husband was gone from the earth. And so was all of Anne's money.

For awhile, the sitting room upstairs in the Wilmington house became a tiny encased world, with her chaise lounge, the wicker tray with a different pattern of her forty sets of breakfast china on it each morning, and her desk with its piles of mail from the Library Board, the DuPont Gardens Foundation, Charity-this, Charity-that. Between charities, life became a frantic search for Lourdes. A trip to Switzerland for acupuncture. "May I tell you, doctor." She'd raised her head and studied the sterile young blond whose skin seemed as starched as his white coat. "I have done a great deal of needlepoint in my life. And I find that after one has pricked oneself enough times, it no longer hurts. I suspect that is the theory behind acupuncture."

A trip to Mayo's. "There's this new doctor, with this theory that . . ." and off she'd flown, only to be pinned to the bed like a moth in a collection, and subjected to a series of exhausting tests.

"You have rheumatoid arthritis," the mustached doctor announced in a no-nonsense voice as his bevy of young interns stared down at her like a Boy Scout troop inspecting their Eagle Badge project.

"Brilliant," she had replied. "To think I've paid $7,000 to be poked in every orifice and then told something I've known for years. It is a miracle of modern medical science."

And she returned to the one cure that always worked:

warm gin. She was staring into a glass of it the day she heard the car on the snow-packed street, cracking as it stopped in the drive, the footsteps crunching toward the door. She knew those footsteps in her darkest sleep.

"You're going to ruin your liver with those," the doctor had said, opening his worn bag.

"Is that a promise?"

"Lexey Jane, there's a health spa outside Dallas. I want you to go for a few days. They can't cure a thing, but they can put you back into some sort of health. The more you drink, the worse off you are."

"Do you have this curse I've got inside my bones?"

"No."

"Then don't give me advice."

"Go. It's warm down there. Get out of this damnable snow."

"What's the name of it?"

"The Terrarium."

"Hah!" she'd winced as the needle jabbed in her. "For potted plants!"

But she went. Another garden. Only of a different variety. A garden of endings *and* beginnings. She'd left her tiny world of chaise lounges and wicker breakfast trays, stacks of charity mail, and, thousands of miles away, she found the German husband who had murdered her dear Anne. Then almost got herself killed trying to save the Penn Central from bankruptcy.

"They keep stealing my trains!" Her eyes popped open as her fist came down on the imperishable blue woolen seat of the Santa Fe Chief. A little puff of dust arose. On the floor, she saw the letter from the petite woman with shining eyes and carts of books who had told her, "I will love this house as you have."

Lexey Jane watched it vibrate toward her toe. With vicious determination, she clutched her cane and stabbed the letter with the sharp ferrule, skewering her sorrow and Rebecca West's. Now the house would be gone. And in its place a cardboard and Tinker Toy construction. It would be ugly, of course. Just as they had stolen all the trains, the world had forgotten how to construct a building with heart and soul.

She wrenched the letter from the tip of the cane and stuffed it back into her purse. "Yes, all the good things will soon be gone." At that moment, the train flung itself around a curve. "Oh!" she cried aloud. Through the soot-stained window, mountains billowed up in the distance, like waves tossed by some heavy gale. "Oh!" she cried again, squinting and peering through the smudged glass. "There are lots of good and beautiful things left!"

The door of her compartment opened. "Lamy!" a voice sang out.

"Ah." She smiled. She'd waited a long time to hear that word, the name of the priest whom the Vatican had chosen to bring the divine cause to this desolate, savage land. He had come with dusty robes and an irrepressible spirit, enduring—for God's sake—in that spirit, for the pains of the flesh had been severe.

The train heaved to a stop, hovered in a tremble, then lurched backward, flinging Lexey Jane against the armrest. She clamped her teeth. "Bishop Lamy," she whispered a scream, "I don't care if you did ride out here in 1851 on the back of a mule. Your bones couldn't have hurt any more than mine!" She waited a moment for the swaying inside her to settle, then gripped the meerschaum-headed cane and tottered down the corridor.

"Oh!"

Something hard as concrete attacked her from the rear and with a clanking noise banged into the back of her legs. She crumpled forward. From behind, an arm hurled around her waist to catch her. The excruciating strength of it crushed against her ribs.

"I'm terribly sorry!"

Lexey Jane steadied herself with the cane, turned and looked up into a distressed bearded face. "Young man," she said, as she glared at him sternly to hide the wrench of pain, "it seems there are only two of us disboarding, so there's no reason to throw both of us from the train."

He flushed and mumbled another apology, picking up the suitcase which had hit her legs and sent her flying. Suddenly, he was on the platform below reaching both arms up to her. "I'll make it up to you." He grinned charmingly.

Lexey Jane held a gloved hand forward. He took it, and she was surprised by the enormous size of his hand. He lifted her like a feather and set her down beside her luggage. She looked at him again. He was not really as young as she'd first thought; middle-age was hidden beneath the beard. He smiled and she noticed that the creases on his brow were actually two long scars, one slightly misplaced over the bridge of his nose. "Thank you, young man."

"I'm truly sorry about knocking you down."

Lexey Jane brushed it aside and leaned slightly on her cane, watching the train pull out. The ground trembled beneath her, and she waited for the throb to move up her old arthritic legs to her heart. When she could no longer see the Chief, Lexey Jane turned and gazed out across the vastness.

At the edge of the small, bricked platform ran a bumpy dirt road. In the distance, on top of a sloping hill, sat a restaurant modeled like a western saloon. "The Legal Tender," the sign read. Next to it, a crumbling adobe house, and to the right an abandoned low concrete building with a row of doors. "Cribs?" she wondered wickedly, for it looked like an old-fashioned brothel, each room with its private entrance opening onto a long, covered porch. No, silly. That's probably where the handymen put up for the night. After all, this was once the end of the line.

"Before they built the spur into Santa Fe in 1880, they used to coach the passengers into town from here," she said to the bearded man. "Now they no longer use the spur, and we're right back to 1880," she said with a laugh.

The man glanced at her. He lifted his suitcase with effort, stepped a small distance from her, and set it down with that strange clanking noise. His eyes scanned the dirt road. "Oh?" he finally said.

"*Stage*coach," she clarified. "I'll bet that was a ride."

He nodded, and turned back toward the road.

Lexey Jane gave an audible "humph" and looked first at a dented pickup parked in front of the one-room station, and then at the driver. He looked back at her, but there was no sign of recognition. The hotel was to send a car for her. But this beat-up, rusty old thing with a hippie at the wheel? She called out to him, "Are you to pick up a passenger?"

"No, lady. My wife works at the Legal Tender. I just came over here to watch the train." He smiled. It was truly a young face, smooth, with long blond hair.

She moved to a wooden bench, sat down, and sighed. Inside the station, she could hear the sounds of closing up. Last train? Only train. In a moment she heard a side door shut, a car somewhere in back start up and head in a swirl of dust down the road. Last train. *Only* train. She squinted at the cloud of dust, certain that out of it would appear the car from the hotel. But it floated, settled, and there was nothing.

She watched the bearded man walk a small circle around his suitcase, then plant his feet on either side of it, shove his hands in his pockets, and lean back as though he'd finally found a suitable position for waiting. She started to introduce herself, but felt too awkward. Besides he was like a statue standing over there at the edge of the platform as if he'd experienced some harsh lesson in patience. The charming smile, the lift from the train? He had abruptly changed into a stranger. She looked back at the pickup. The young man had slumped down in the seat and was watching something in the distance.

Quiet.

It was so quiet. She peered at the scrubby pines on a small knoll and listened. Strange. No birds. She cocked an ear at the silence. In a moment a car will come down that road. It will just roar down that road and gather up my luggage and transport me to a soft bed where my bones can heal.

The sun dropped suddenly behind the mountains. A quick chill made her pull her coat closer around her. She tucked the soft cashmere around her knees. They were quivering. "I'm just chilly," she reassured herself. Nothing to be frightened of out here. Nothing at all.

The bearded man waited in the same unchanging stance. The young hippie had closed his eyes. His head lolled disjointedly against the seat, twisted toward her. Was he watching her? Of course not.

Suddenly, there were no more shadows. Dusk dropped like gray fur around her.

"Is there a telephone?" She jumped at the sound of her own voice jarring the silence. It sounded thin and wavering.

The bearded man slowly turned a grim, tight face toward her. "What? Oh, probably inside the station." His large head pivoted back to the road.

Painfully, Lexey Jane stood and tried the door. Locked. She gasped, turned, and looked across the platform, beyond the dirt road toward the restaurant on the hill. Miles. Endless miles for an arthritic old lady wobbling on the end of a cane. She tapped it irritably on the brick, but neither the bearded man nor the hippie stirred. Far in the distance she heard the groan of a semitruck on a highway. What about all those stories of people lost in the desert, dying from thirst when just over the next hill is civilization and a hot cup of coffee? Oh, posh, Lexey Jane! Julien always says you worry about the wrong things.

Suddenly, the door of the restaurant flew open. A short man with a rigid military back led four octogenarians across the porch and down the hill. He marched ahead of them as if they were a platoon. She could hear him counting out the step as they quickly disappeared up the road. In a blink, the bizarre little group was gone in the distance.

Did I see that? She glanced at the bearded man. He had not moved. I know I saw that! She waited, half-expecting to hear the beat of a Sousa march. Silence.

At least it means there's life up there, she sighed hopefully.

"Young man," she said at last, "would you please go to that restaurant over there and call the hotel for me? The La Fonda Hotel."

He turned to her frowning, as if she'd wrenched him from some task. "Don't worry. If they said they'd send a car for you, they'll send a car." He moved a foot, protectively straddling the suitcase. "There's no phone up there, anyway."

She leaned back against the bench. The hard boards pricked at her backbone. He'd talked to her like an errant child! No phone? No phone in a restaurant? Through the dimness, she squinted at the telephone poles in the distance, at the wires crisscrossing, leading straight to the Legal Tender. Could she be wrong? Did those wires bypass the restaurant? She glanced at the bearded man again, but he was once more plunged into his silent watch. Why would he lie about a telephone?

On the hill a door closed at the restaurant, and a young girl in a white uniform walked across the porch and down the slope, her feet sliding on the loose stones. She crossed the road to the pickup. The hippie's eyes fluttered open and he uncoiled from the seat. "Busy today?" His voice floated through the dark.

"That Sierra bunch hiked out for dinner," the girl answered.

Lexey Jane half-rose from the bench. Her throat struggled with a shout. Last train. Suddenly, the boy leaned out the window and called to her. "Hey, lady! You need a ride to town?"

"Yes!" Lexey Jane jumped at the fright in her voice. What was wrong with her?

The young hippie climbed languidly from the cab and gathered up her luggage. "Hey, mister. You need a ride, too? I think we can squeeze everybody in."

The bearded man threw him a harsh look. "No, no thank you."

With dismay, Lexey Jane saw her Vuitton luggage tossed into the truck bed with old tires and firewood, a mountain of oily tools, a tire jack, several hammers, an ax, and coils of wire. "There. That'll ride back there okay." He walked around to the other door. "Here, let me help you. There's no catch on that side, so I'll have to tie the handle."

The cab door creaked open and lopped to one side on exhausted hinges. The cry escaped Lexey Jane before she could swallow it. Crouching on the seat next to the young girl was an enormous black and white hairy dog. From somewhere behind a torrent of whiskers she felt sharp teeth bared at her. A low growl rumbled across the seat.

"It's okay, Snooker. Move over. Come on, boy, move over," the hippie coaxed. The beast wagged a tail the size of Lexey Jane's arm and moved closer to the young girl crowded in the middle. Lexey Jane crunched in beside them while the hippie tied a frayed rope around the outside handle. "There. That ought to hold you in."

As he started up the truck, Lexey Jane felt a cold, wet nose bury itself in her cheek. She tried moving, but there was simply no room. A warm sandpaper tongue reached around and licked her chin. She turned and was nose to nose with the beast. "Snookerrrr," she warned in a whisper, snapping her eyes at the monster.

As the pickup bumped down the dirt road, Lexey Jane tried looking back, but it was too painful. Through the dust she could see only the dim outline of the bearded man, still in the same pose, watching the cloud kick up behind the rattletrap truck. It bounced and jolted. The loose door at her shoulder banged and shivered. She tried to ask a question, her voice stuttering above the noise, "Do you live in Santa Fe?" and was instantly sorry, for the pickup reared into the air and she bit her tongue on the last word.

"Well, not exactly," the young man replied. The girl beside him was silent. "We live on the other side of Santa Fe. In a pyramid."

"In a pyramid!" Lexey Jane shrieked. The pickup hit a bump and she flew upward. Frantically, she grabbed the shredded strap hanging above the window.

"Yeah. Those chambers in the pyramids in Egypt were healing chambers, not graves for the dead. You read Edgar Cayce, lady?" He flung the words at her like a threat.

"Young man." Lexey Jane's breath came in gasps. She bounced around between Snooker and the precarious door. It beat against her hip bone in chaotic agony. "I'll have you know my father used Edgar Cayce's extraordinary talents in drilling an oil well!"

So abruptly did the old pickup clatter to a jarring, thudding halt that Lexey Jane barely had time to brace herself from flying through the windshield. The boy leaned forward excitedly, "You're kidding!"

"No, I am most certainly not. He was drilling a well down in Texas, and he lost the tool—you know, the drilling bit. And they couldn't find it. Fishing, they call it. So my father called Edgar Cayce in Chicago and asked him to go into a trance over the telephone and help him find that lost tool." Lexey Jane took a deep breath, grateful for the sudden inertia of the old truck. "He did. And they did. And he'd never seen an oil well in his life. After that, my father brought Cayce out to Texas for a trip around the field. Now, young man, if you don't mind, I am extremely tired and would like to go to my hotel. Slowly."

"Fantastic! Annie? Did you hear what she just said?" But the girl stared straight ahead. With difficulty, he started up the truck. It bounced forward, then settled into a cacophonic rhythm down a narrow street. "I guess sometimes it pays to be old," the boy went on. "I mean, you can remember things like that."

The dog planted a giant foot on her thigh. She gasped with pain. "I guess there has to be some compensation," she sighed, struggling with the paw.

"You're on the old Santa Fe Trail now," the boy called out brightly.

"And I am in a stagecoach, and you live in a pyramid," she whispered. *Julien will never believe this. It's too bizarre.* In the dusk, the low, sand-colored buildings huddled close to the side of the road, to the earth, to each other. She could see ladders leaning against walls, leading to upstairs rooms. I've lost my way, she thought suddenly. I am on a back road in Jerusalem. In a moment I will hear the bells for evening prayers.

"Hey, Annie! Look! Isn't that a flying saucer?" The boy slowed down at a stoplight.

Disregarding her pain, Lexey Jane crouched down and peered out of the cracked window. In the sky hung a luminous, cigar-shaped object on end.

"That is the television antenna on the hospital roof," the girl answered through clenched teeth.

Undaunted, the boy pulled his head back in the window. "You do see a lot of 'em out here. It's the magnetic field in this place. They think this whole area was once a pole, you know, an axis, like the North Pole. Before the earth shifted."

"Then I would appreciate your driving me to the hotel before we become permanently attached to this intersection." Lexey Jane wearily fumbled in her purse for some money to coax him through the green light.

"They're studying us," he went on, trying to start the engine, "like cattle."

"Studying us?" Lexey Jane turned skeptically toward him and met the hairy monster beside her, eye to eye. "Who is studying us?"

The boy leaned forward over the steering wheel and smiled winsomely at her. "Venusians."

Lexey Jane moved her lips as if chewing on her sarcasm. "Oh, of course. From the evening star." Be nice, Lexey Jane. One does not insult the stagecoach driver, else one does not arrive at the inn.

The boy just grinned. He tried to start the truck. It

groaned and shook against loose metal beneath the floor-board. He tried it again. This time, nothing.

"Damn you!" Annie growled.

"Now don't get upset. I'll have it in a minute." The boy pumped the gas pedal until the air reeked of fumes, then got out and opened the hood, which like the fenders had been welded into a patchwork quilt. Suddenly, it flopped back against the windshield and the boy disappeared inside the engine. It was uncomfortably quiet inside the cab. Lexey Jane's right side next to the door was freezing, her left side was on fire from the heat of the giant dog. She could hear the girl gulping great angry mouthfuls of air.

"I'm going to kill him. Someday I'm going to kill him." Annie doubled her fist and pounded it against the dashboard. Then she leaped into the street and began shaking her fist at the body half-buried beneath the hood. "You told me you'd fixed it!" she screamed. She had one of those scrubbed, plain faces, no cosmetics, and it was pulled tight into a frightening snarl. "You liar!" Her eyes darted around wildly. "You have to put on your little show for everyone you meet." Her voice dropped to a surly warning. "You get this damned thing going, do you hear me?" She rose again to hysterical pitch. "Do you hear me?"

The head rose up slowly from behind the hood. "Annie, calm down. I'll get it started in a minute. It always starts"—he managed a grin—"eventually."

"If . . . if there's a phone somewhere near, I can call a taxi." Lexey Jane discovered her voice was three notes higher than Annie's hysteria. She tried to move. A leaden weight struck her in the lap. "You are crushing my pelvis, you monster!" she snapped at the dog. He had pinned her to the seat. Desperately, she reached for the rope looped through the door. A hard knot. It would take a screwdriver to untie that knot. Her crippled fingers would never make it.

Annie flung her a quick, hateful glance through the window, and pounded her fist on the fender. Just as abruptly, she turned and resolutely folded her arms, staring at a station wagon coming from the opposite direction.

"There's your taxi," she said, and walked straight into the path of the oncoming car. The station wagon began honking, and inched its way across the intersection.

Lexey Jane could now see the sign on the side: La Fonda Hotel. "Here I am! I'm right here," she called, reaching an arm across the dog. A wet, sawtooth pain clamped around her wrist. "Ah!" Lexey Jane whirled on the dog. "What- . . . Help!"

The boy dashed around the side of the truck. "Snooker!" he ordered in a voice of such brutal strength that a shudder whipped through Lexey Jane. Snooker released his hold. Across the street, she could hear Annie talking to the driver of the station wagon. ". . . thought you weren't coming . . . Jerry offered her a ride . . ."

In a sudden flurry, Lexey Jane saw her luggage thrown into the back of the station wagon, while someone ripped away the door at her side. With a horrible crunching shriek, it fell open, and she was toppling to the pavement with arms reaching at her from every direction.

Now she was peering into a tiny face engulfed in a mammoth raccoon coat.

"So sorry, Mrs. Pelazoni," a whispery feminine voice said. "But I was late coming from the airport. Here, let me help you. Your cane?"

The one thing Lexey Jane detested was losing her poise. But from the moment she'd arrived in this place, beginning with her flying exit from the train to this switch in the middle of the Santa Fe trail, she'd had her sense of balance and decorum pulled out from under her. Now, in the street, she fumbled nervously through her purse. "I want to pay you for your trouble," she said as she handed some bills to the young man.

"Aw, lady, I can't take that."

Lexey Jane rapped her cane on the pavement. "My name is Lexey Jane, and yes, you can take it!"

The boy took a step backward. "Okay . . . Lexey . . Lexey Jane. But I still can't take that."

Suddenly, a hand reached out of the dark and snatched the bills from her fingers. "Yes, we can," Annie said with cold anger.

Lexey Jane felt herself gently guided toward the station wagon and into the front seat. At first she thought Snooker had climbed in behind the wheel. But it was the mountainous raccoon coat. "I'll turn around and give you a push," it was saying out the window.

The station wagon nosed up expertly behind the pickup, then nudged the dangling rear bumper down the street. In a moment, a fusillade of blue smoke poured from the exhaust in front of them. Through the haze, Lexey Jane saw Snooker raise his enormous head from the seat and glare at her out the back window.

The raccoon coat sighed. "Did you try to call?"

"There was no phone."

"Oh, yes. There's one in the station and at the restaurant."

Lexey Jane smoothed the paw print from her coat. "Thought so," she muttered.

"There were supposed to be two passengers. Did anyone else get off at Lamy?"

"Yes, a bearded man. Most unpleasant," she added.

"Oh? Well, we're so close to the hotel, I'll run you there and then go back for him. Uh . . . did you know that couple?"

"No, seemed nice, though. At least the young man . . ."

"That was most unwise, Mrs. Pelazoni. Total strangers, hippies, you know. Flag you down and then rob you."

Lexey Jane looked at the girl. The tiny Geraldine Chaplin face was pretty beneath a film of fatigue. The raccoon coat that reached to her ankles had fallen open and beneath it glittered an embroidered and jeweled cocktail dress of thirties vintage. Lexey Jane blinked. She would certainly have to redefine her idea of a hippie out here in Santa Fe.

The girl turned and smiled. "I didn't mean to startle you. But you must be careful."

Sudden tears stung Lexey Jane's eyes. Memory tears. This girl swaddled in fur sounded so much like Anne.

"My name is Shiela McCarthy," she said softly.

"Thank goodness."

The girl laughed. "What does that mean?"

"I was beginning to think no one out here had a name. You are the first person to initiate a proper introduction."

She laughed again, a nice gurgling sound. "Oh, I have a name, all right. "Irish-to-the-bone Shiela McCarthy, M.A., Ph. D., sometime author." She threw a quick grin at Lexey Jane as she maneuvered the car down a thin, winding street with flat-roofed adobes, ". . . and chauffeur."

"It's going to look rather odd on a tombstone."

Shiela tilted her head inside the fur collar and laughed openly. "Not in Santa Fe. Yesterday a doctor of physics fixed my toilet, if you can believe it."

"A friend?"

"No. A plumber."

"Incredible. What would make him want to do that?"

The girl flashed a quick, tired smile at her. "He's a runner."

"A runner?"

"The place is full of them. Runners. All running from something."

"But from what . . . ?"

"The great American dream of success, mostly. There's a hot-dog vendor in Taos who used to be a Wall Street broker, an ex-vice-president of IBM who runs a candle factory, an heir to Matson shipping lines who shoes horses . . ." She chuckled. "Sort of turns you upside down for awhile. The old measuring stick won't work—money, prestige, position. Here, it's what you do, what talent you have." She was silent for a moment. "And there are runners who are running from themselves." She whipped the car next to a curb. "Well, here we are," she announced brightly, "the La Fonda. The end of the trail."

Lexey Jane looked at the thick white adobe walls leaning slightly inward, like a pyramid with the top sliced off, she thought in surprise. "So this is the old Harvey House," she said wistfully.

"You've been here before?" Shiela was reaching for her luggage.

"No, no. Always wanted to come. I like the history of the place."

"So do I. Oldest town in the United States. I think they date it somewhere around 1598."

"Really? St. Augustine, Florida, will not be happy to hear that."

"I know." Shiela smiled, setting the luggage on the walk. "They fight back and forth about it all the time. Really doesn't matter, though, does it?"

Climbing slowly from the car, Lexey Jane quickly studied the girl. Something in her voice revealed that she had happened upon other things in life more important than the date of a city. Something hazardous to the soul. Lexey Jane quietly pulled some bills from her purse and laid them on the front seat. "I'll pretend I didn't see that." The soft voice was suddenly hard and flat.

Lexey Jane gave a brusque "humph" to hide her emotions. "Nonsense! That must have been left by someone else."

Shiela smiled and shook her head. "I'll get a bellhop for you, and then I'd better scoot back to Lamy and find that other passenger. Adios."

Lexey Jane watched the station wagon disappear around a corner. "Ph.D., chauffeur, pyramids, . . . incredible."

"What's that, señora?"

Startled, Lexey Jane faced the bellhop. "Oh, nothing. Nothing."

She followed him through the heavy wooden doors, her cane tapping on the clay-tiled floor, up some steps, and . . . Lexey Jane halted in amazement. Beneath the heavy, carved beams and lintels, leaning or squatting against the thick pillars in the middle of the lobby, were *Indians*. Old, rusty, lined faces with long black braids falling over the blankets wrapped around their shoulders. "Indians," she gasped.

"Oh yes, señora, and for fifty cents you can take their picture."

A smartly dressed woman clicked past them in high heels and was lost immediately in a shifting forest of leather-fringed jackets and bluejeans—bluejean suits, bluejean dresses, bluejean skirts—a sea of denim. Around her swirled the soft words of Spanish, the thick accent of German, the nasal sing-song of Japanese. The manager at the desk greeted her in clipped British. "Ah, Mrs. Pelazoni. So nice to welcome you to Santa Fe." But from the shrug of his shoulders, Lexey Jane knew that somehow West London had merged completely with mañana.

"This way, señora." The bellhop started down a long, wide hall lined with cavernous fireplaces. Lexey Jane found herself riding up in a mirrored elevator, her frazzled reflection winking at her from a thousand facets. In her room, she smiled at the wildly painted bed and chest. Gaudy birds flew across the drawers, bolts of Navaho lightning zigzagged over the headboard. In the bathroom a newly installed chrome handle had been plastered into the wall by the tub, the security she needed. She turned and inspected the tiled lavatory and mirror. They were almost hidden behind a spiderweb of gimcrack wiring. "Probably wired by a poet," she smiled to herself. It did have a certain aesthetic appeal—lacework over the whitewashed wall. "Is that safe?" she asked the porter.

"Si, si, señora," he answered with that confidence which had so maddened her in Europe every time she'd received a wrong direction.

"You're sure?"

"Si-i-i-i, señora."

And Lexey Jane caught herself shrugging as the porter left. Shrugging! She laughed. "It doesn't take long. I've been here ten minutes and I'm shrugging like a native."

She sat on the edge of the bed and, for the first time, allowed her painful shoulders to slump. She studied the phone at her side. "You've got to call Peaches." She listened to her own gravelly voice hang in the air for a moment. "Trepidation. That's the word, Lexey Jane. You are afraid to call her." She lifted the receiver and quickly placed a call to New York, waiting to hear Julien's precise, reassuring voice.

It kept ringing. She dialed his office.

"Hello."

"You said to call when I arrived."

"Lexey Jane! You're almost two hours late! What happened? Didn't you get my messages? I've been ringing your room for the past hour . . ."

"Julien!" she interrupted him excitedly. "You can't believe what it's like! I've met two people who live in a pyramid, been chauffeured here by a Ph.D., physics professors are plumbers, and there are real live Indians in the lobby. Julien, when they put 'land of enchantment' on the license plates, they didn't just mean the scenery."

Julien puffed a laugh at her ebullience. "Sounds a bit bizarre."

"I knew you'd say that," she sighed, a little dismayed that Julien never offered her any surprises. Well, almost never.

"Have you talked to . . . uh, your friend . . ." Although Julien had been her portfolio manager and legal counselor for years, he could not bring himself to say that absurd first name. ". . . Mrs. Mueller?"

"Peaches?" Lexey Jane laughed. "No, I will right away, though. I promised to call you first."

There was a pause. "Where did she get that name? Surely her parents didn't . . ."

"Left over from the twenties, Julien. I've never told you what *my* nickname was."

"Should I be grateful?"

"Duzey. After the Duesenberg."

"The automobile? I don't understand."

"Because in my day it was the best," she answered tersely. "And so was I."

"You still are." She heard him chuckle.

"Not in the same way, I'm afraid." She rubbed a hand along her aching thighs.

"You're putting it off, aren't you? Calling Mrs. Mueller."

He'd caught her by surprise. "Yes."

"Just remember"—Julien's voice was stern—"you don't have to tell her anything tonight."

"I know." But Julien didn't know Peaches Mueller like she did. "Have you called TC yet?" she asked.

"I've been putting that off, too. I dislike being solely responsible for starting a world revolution. And that's what could happen, you know."

"I'll see that you have a place in Red Square."

"It's not funny."

"I'm sorry. Julien? What are you doing at the office this time of night?"

She heard a long, frustrated explosion of air. "I am going over these certificates. I still can't believe it. The man is the most superb artist I've ever encountered."

"Ah, that's an accolade I'm afraid he will never get to hear."

"Lexey Jane, I want you to be careful. You talked me in to letting you go. Now that you're there, try to follow my instructions. Don't do anything, do you understand, *anything* without checking with me first."

"Oh, Julien." She chuckled. "You know counterfeiters are souls interested in Sunday outings and baseball and domestic things like that. Not a vicious lot at all."

"What makes you so sure?"

"They're artists, aren't they? Artists don't go around killing people."

"If you are stabbed with an engraving needle, don't say I didn't warn you."

Lexey Jane laughed aloud. "Very good, Julien. Very good." Staid, pompous, dour Julien *could* surprise her now and then.

She hung up and straightened her back, pressing her hand against her lower spine. "I won't call her at all," she spoke to the phone. "I'll wait till morning and then . . ." But the thing was already screaming at her from the bedside table. Reluctantly, she picked up the receiver.

"Duzey! You're here! Can I see you tonight? It's still early."

Lexey Jane squeezed her eyes shut, then opened them and smiled back at the thin, high voice on the line. "Bit exhausted tonight. Train ride and all. Peaches?" She would use diversion. "The lobby of this hotel is filled with blankets and braids. Real live Indians! Just like in all those Gary Cooper movies!"

Peaches laughed. "Well, the last time I was in New York, it was all nipples and wrinkled cotton, and I was just as amazed."

"Well, dear, I'll call you tomorrow," Lexey Jane added quickly.

"Duzey!" The voice shrieked at her. "You didn't come all the way to Santa Fe for a visit. I know you. You were never happy unless you were doing two things at once. Tell me. What is it?"

"I'll talk to you tomorrow, Peaches."

"It's the TC stock, isn't it?"

"Peaches!" Lexey Jane pounded the bed with her fist in exasperation.

Peaches gave a gasping titter. "You didn't tell me, Duzey. I guessed. Julien was angry with me, but I didn't want to wash all the old dirty linen with him, so I figured he sent you, or someone from TC sent you—what's wrong? Is it counterfeit?" She chuckled.

"You knew all the time?"

"You mean it *is* counterfeit?" The voice clanged hysterically against Lexey Jane's ear.

"Oh, my God." Lexey Jane squirmed on the bed. She was joking! And she joked correctly! "Peaches, listen to me. Peaches!" All she could hear was a croaking rattle over the phone. "Peaches!"

"I can't get . . . my . . . breath."

Lexey Jane listened helplessly to the long, rasping intakes. "Are you all right?"

"It's the irony of it!" Peaches screamed. "I wanted to show up at the board meeting owning a million dollars of their damned company. My company, Duzey—it was once *my* company!"

"Peaches," Lexey Jane soothed, "it's too late. All that's in the past. It's an old battle."

"Hah! You think I'm going to lose a second time? Not on your life, Duzey. Not on your life."

"Who sold it to you?"

"You'll meet him tomorrow. Come for lunch. I'll have him here."

"Peaches, I don't think you should play games with someone who has sold you counterfeit stock," Lexey Jane warned. An explosion of coughing ripped her eardrum. "Peaches, who is your doctor? I'm going to call him right this minute. You sound terrible."

"I am in excellent health, Duzey. Excellent health. You have the map to my house?"

"Yes . . ."

"Good. I'll see you at twelve o'clock."

Lexey Jane looked at the receiver a long time as if expecting another phlegmatic explosion to come from it. The dialtone buzzed, and she put it back in the cradle.

She was shaking. Damn! Should she call Julien? No.

He'd only order her back to New York. She rolled her tongue around her mouth. She felt sour and doltish all over. She reached across the bed for her cane and limped into the bathroom. Pulling one of the electrical cords away from the mirror, she looked at her frazzled reflection. The hairdresser had made her look like a head of cauliflower. Turning, she looked at her humped shoulders and with agonizing effort, straightened them. "There is only one thing that will restore me to human shape," she said aloud. "Just one gin."

The elevator was self-service. She waited for it to reach the lobby before starting to panic. She hated these mute elevators. Always afraid of catching her cane in the closing door behind her and rising to the top story like Mary Poppins. The moment the door slid open, she spurted through, ramming directly into a very hard body.

"Oh, I'm terribly sorry!" The man grabbed her before her legs buckled.

She looked up into the cheerful face of the bearded man from the train. "There *is* a phone at the restaurant," she snapped, banging down her cane.

"What?" His eyes popped open.

"A phone. There is a phone at that restaurant in Lamy. And you knew it all the time."

"I'm sorry. I didn't know it . . . I . . . look, why don't I buy you a drink and make up for all those bruises I must have given you."

"Lead the way."

Without moving, he grinned down at her. "I will if you'll remove your cane from the toe of my shoe. You have just perforated my only pair of loafers."

Lexey Jane heard herself laughing. "I'm Lexey Jane Pelazoni."

"And I'm Mannie Ringer." He took her arm, propelling her toward the bar.

"Are you a tourist, Mr. Ringer?"

"No. I'm moving here. Going to buy a house tomorrow."

"Are you a runner?"

He whirled on her. "A what?"

"A runner. That girl who drives the limousine said people ran to Santa Fe to escape something. Are you running from something?"

"Not anymore. I came here to be an artist."

Lexey Jane's uncertain foot halted. He'd answered the question with a fresh arrogance to it, a startling determination that bordered on menace. She started to ask what kind of artist, when she saw the two men watching them from a doorway. One of them stood in a stiff military stance; the other looked oddly familiar. Somewhere she'd seen him before. In a book. Somewhere in a book she had seen that face.

At 11:47 P.M. on March 1, Mannie Ringer unlocked his hotel room door and quickly shut it behind him. Then he stood a moment staring down at the envelope that had been slipped under the door. He took a step backward as if it were a live grenade. Puzzled, he picked it up and turned it in his hand, tapping a corner against his palm. Suddenly, he bolted across the room, flung open the closet door, and reached for his suitcase. Still locked. He opened it. Everything in its place.

"It doesn't make sense," he mumbled. He didn't know a soul in Santa Fe. Hesitantly, he slashed the envelope with his finger and unfolded the message:

Just how good is the vintage?

A torrent of heat flashed through him. He crumpled the

note and hurled it across the room in fury. "What the shit is going on?" He threw himself back on the bed, folded his arms under his head, and glared at the heavy timber beams running across the ceiling.

The two guys in the bar. They were obviously watching him and Lexey Jane. But which one? Which one had left the note? The one with the strange, flattened face, or the little dapper guy in a tee-shirt and jeans? Both? "Goddamn," he moaned, and rolled on his side. "Jesus Christ!" He beat the bed until dust from the spread filled his nostrils.

Or was it Lexey Jane? What was that bit about his being a "runner"? And she is rich. Very rich. He spotted it in her clothes, her luggage, the way she walked. She could move easily in those faraway circles of wealth. But an old crippled dame? Why would anyone send someone like that? Yet she had been on the train.

"Coincidence, Mannie," he told himself.

"Bullshit!" the other half of him warned. "You're getting sloppy in your middle-age."

"No, you're getting senile."

In the middle of this debate he finally fell into a fitful sleep. Somewhere in the distance he heard a siren. No. Something else. He rolled over and opened his eyes. He'd left all the lights on. And his phone was ringing. He glanced at his watch. One-thirty in the morning.

"Hello?"

"Who is the old lady?"

"What?" Mannie rubbed his face hard with his hand, trying to beat himself awake.

"Who is the old lady?"

"Who the hell is this?"

He heard a chuckle. "You don't know?" The man sounded pleased. "It's Iris. Is she in this with you?"

"What?" Mannie was sitting upright.

"The old lady."

"What the hell are you doing here?" Mannie felt his insides sinking. Best thing to do was hang up. He had the receiver halfway toward the cradle when he heard a snap of teeth.

"Doesn't matter now. She got herself killed," said the voice. The receiver clicked.

"What?" Mannie screamed into the phone. "What did you say?" He was still shouting at the buzzing in his ear.

He hung up and sat numbly, running his hand through his hair until it rose like bristles from his head.

"Oh, my God!" He grabbed the phone and dialed a number. It rang only twice. He heard the gravelly voice answer.

"Lexey Jane?"

"Yes, Mannie. Is that you?"

"Yeah." He was kicking himself for being so stupid. "I just . . . just got worried about you. Wanted to know if you were okay."

"I'm fine."

But Mannie heard the curious lilt in her voice. And she was too smart a broad not to ponder a call from a half-stranger at one-thirty in the morning.

Chapter Two

After he had overcome the impulse to crumple the starched paper and throw it across his office, Julien Strauss pulled the high-intensity lamp closer. Not in all his years of legal work, in all his dealings in the shadow world of finance, had he seen anything like this. With complete precision, he duplicated what he had done three days ago when he first received the negotiable stock from Mrs. Peaches Mueller.

Under the hard light, he checked the serial number. 66666. Only it wasn't. The certificate was upside down. With the same motion he'd made three days ago, and a hundred times since, he turned the certificate around. 99999. A simple gesture. Turn the paper around, right side up. Yet, if he hadn't noticed that the numbers were upside down, it was possible he never would have realized what he was looking at now.

Three days ago, just as he had started to record the number before placing the stock in the vault, the memory that had startled Harvard clicked. Lexey Jane had 10,000 shares of Transcontinental Communications—a stock certificate numbered 99999! Surely there was a mistake. He could remember thinking that, but not trusting it. His memory rarely failed him. Rarely? Never. He had opened the vault in his office and pulled out the thick folder file of Lexey Jane's stocks. There it was. The same certificate. The same number.

"It's forged!" he had shouted. "She's purchased a million dollars of nothing!" An error in her judgment, a scratchy situation. A problem. But certainly not one that would shake the foundations of Wall Street.

That's what he thought then.

He had pulled Lexey Jane's certificate and placed it on the desk, then huddled over them both, examining them until hot tears of strain blurred his exhausted eyes. "It can't be. It just can't be. It's impossible."

Experts had agreed for years that no well-designed and executed certificate done by the intaglio process could be exactly imitated. And most listed companies used not one engraved plate, but *two*. One for the border which had to be in color, and the other for the vignette, the title and text. Well, Julien thought scornfully, the experts should see this.

It was pure effrontery. The ultimate insult. What kind of pompous arrogance did it take to counterfeit one certificate for 10,000 shares of TC? Certain to be scrutinized by the bank official, the transfer agent . . . by *him*.

Again, he lifted the large magnifying glass over the paper. The picture, or vignette, was the most difficult to imitate. In forgeries, the Greek gods and goddesses usually lacked fine detail, and the artwork was muddy with no range of tone, no delicate skin tones on the figure. But this fleshy Greek goddess traipsing along a rainbow spanning two engraved continents was a masterpiece. The inks had to be blended with extreme care to produce just that off-shade of green.

The scrolls twining around both certificates whirled at him beneath the bright, focused light. He closed his eyes.

In the ball of light still caught behind his eyelids, he could see Lexey Jane standing in his office only the day before yesterday. "I'm confiding in you because you don't talk and you don't get excited," he'd told her. "Your friend Mrs. Mueller has purchased a counterfeit, I think."

"What do you mean, *you think*?" she'd asked.

"I don't know which is the counterfeit," he had mumbled, "hers or yours."

"Why of course, the counterfeit is Peaches'," she'd snapped back with that maddening certainty of hers.

"How do you know?" he'd almost shouted.

"You mean you don't know?"

"Know what?"

"Someone wanted a million dollars badly. And they found the way to get it. They knew Peaches' soft underbelly."

"What does that mean?" Julien remembered doubling his fists, which was unlike him.

"It was one of those shootouts . . . or shootups, I never can remember which—a family feud, Julien. National Communications was the mother company of Transcontinental . . ."

"I know, I know."

". . . owned by the Lambertons," she went on calmly. "When Peaches married Freddie Mueller, she insisted he be included on the board." Her dark eyes rolled mischievously. "Peaches' brother called Freddie Mueller something unmentionable. And Peaches shouted back some rather unspeakable insults. The upshot was that the Lambertons bought Peaches outright, then passed a resolution that she never be able to own any company stock . . . and they all lived unhappily ever after."

"But . . . National merged with Transcontinental . . . it's on the exchange. Anyone can buy it!" he spluttered.

Two eyebrows shot across his desk. "Someone . . ." Lexey Jane chewed the corner of her lip. "Someone is still honoring that resolution. *Or* Peaches hasn't tried to buy any TC stock until someone came to her with this negotiable certificate." She gave a little bob of her gray head. "Someone knew her soft spot, someone with the knowledge of counterfeiting, and got himself a real live million dollars." She put her gloved hand resolutely on the white head of her cane. "*That's* how I know her stock is the counterfeit."

And then he'd allowed her to convince him that she should not only deliver the news to Peaches Mueller, but perhaps trace the counterfeiter through her friend.

Lexey Jane had that distant, dreamy look on her face which always frightened Julien. "I'll take the train."

"That will take two days!"

"Ah." She'd raised a finger at him. "This is one time where speed is not to our advantage."

And she was right. His hand wanted to crawl at a snail's pace toward the phone call he had to make; he was in no real hurry to shatter the pillars of a world market and his own reputation along with it.

He reached for the phone, drew his hand away. Kathryn, clever Kathryn, would zero in on what he had been trying to ignore. What if Lexey Jane's stock *was* counterfeit? What if he, Julien Strauss, wizard extraordinaire, had picked up a forged certificate and cheated his best client, one of his closest friends, out of one million dollars? It was intimidating, embarrassing, and above all, humiliating—an emotion Julien did not like to admit existed in his mind.

"Neither one can be a forgery." He paced the office. "TC Corporation has made a mistake. They've printed two identical series of numbers." He heaved a sigh. He had never known this to happen before. Certainly not in a blue-chip, gold-bonded international concern like Transcontinental Communications. But . . . he reached for the phone again . . . there is a first time for everything. Or at least, Lexey Jane thinks so. Let's hope to God there is.

He started to dial the number, then, hung up. He had to call Kathryn Wyler. And Kathryn Wyler was one of the most beautiful, intelligent women he'd ever met. Her honors from Harvard had propelled her to the top of one of the world's largest corporations. There was one problem. Kathryn Wyler scared the hell out of him. She was *too* smart. He took a deep breath and dialed again.

"Hello." It was a soft, velvet voice.

"Julien Strauss here."

"And Kathryn Wyler here," she teased gently.

"Kathryn, I need to discuss a problem with you involving TC. Is it too late for you to meet me in town for a drink?"

"Oh, Julien, I just live on 38th. Why don't you come over here?"

He hesitated.

She picked up quickly on the silence. "Don't be scared, Julien. Just because I'm a woman, and a black one at that, I won't hurt you."

Julien gulped. "All right," he answered quickly, and was immediately sorry as he hung up. Meeting Kathryn in her apartment put her on home ground. Not wise at all in this kind of battle.

He folded the certificates and put them in his inside pocket. Outside a thin mist was falling, turning the sky above the city a pale violet. "Marvelous what beauty a mixture of neon and pollution can produce," Julien thought as he hailed a cab. Suddenly, his hand smacked against the folded papers inside his suit coat. Another product of modern technology. But this one had not produced any lavender haze over a city. This botched mess was a horror.

Almost afraid to breathe, his nostrils tightened. The old ache slowly began to creep through his feet. He moved his toes as the cab pulled up in front of an apartment house, but it wouldn't go away. It was the pain of double-time. At least, that's what he had called it at Harvard as he walked back and forth over the Anderson Bridge across the Charles River, forcing his feet and brain to go faster and faster. From the Business School at Soldier's Field where presidents of corporations are manufactured, to Harvard Yard in Cambridge where Presidents of the United States are created, he had soaked up the knowledge of both worlds, then embarked as a counselor in the tempestuous love affair between the two. Softly, unobtrusively, he had become the muse and mentor of both sides. "Ask Julien Strauss. He never makes a mistake."

He climbed slowly from the cab and walked up the steps of the apartment house. The pain in his feet grew more intense. He rang the bell, and heard locks sliding back with an explosive rattle.

"You have just brightened my evening," Kathryn sang out as she ushered him through a foyer into a large, brightly colored room. "Here, let me take your coat. You're all wet."

Nervously, Julien took the folded papers from his pocket.
"That the business?" she asked, eyeing them. "At least let
me fix us a drink first. You look like you need one."

Shifting his weight from one foot to the other, he
watched her caramel hands reach into an ice bucket. "You
do that with great efficiency," he sighed, "like everything
else."

"I'd prefer you told me I've got nice legs." She grinned
and handed him his drink. "But I'll settle for efficiency.
From Julien Strauss, I know it's a high compliment."

"I'll bet you didn't make it to the top of TC on your legs."

"No." She smiled slowly. "And I didn't make it on
efficiency either. I'm a black woman, Julien. I appeal to everyone's guilty conscience."

"You underestimate yourself."

"No. I just estimate the world," she chuckled.

He followed her into the living room. Sitting on the divan, she glanced at him. "You look like you're in pain, Julien. Why don't you take off your shoes and put your feet
up?"

Damn. The intuition of women. This was going to be
more difficult that he thought.

"Let's see what you've got clutched in your sweaty
hand," she said, and nodded as he loosened his shoelaces.

Carefully, he unfolded the certificates and placed them
on Kathryn's lap. "Do you notice anything strange about
these?"

Kathryn calmly sipped her drink and examined the papers without touching them. "What we've got here, Julien,
is a case of forgery. The serial numbers are identical."

"Precisely. Would you please tell me which one is the
forgery?"

Kathryn quickly picked one up. "This one . . . no"—she
laid it back down—"this one . . . no . . . I . . . Julien!"

She turned to him, her brown eyes popping. "That's pretty gutsy. *One* certificate for 10,000 shares!"

She grabbed them and held them up to the lamp. "It's remarkable! It's absolutely remarkable!" She turned to him calmly. "But an expert would know the difference. He could tell."

"Kathryn, I've had the same training as an SEC officer, and I can't tell. I've measured the rainbow. I've measured the staff in her hand. Usually, this is where a discrepancy will show itself. But by all accounts, these are identical."

Kathryn held them to the light again. "Look at the lines in this gal's hair. And look at the detail in her robe! I . . . " she turned. "I don't know what to think."

"I don't either. But I think you'll understand why I came to you first instead of the SEC."

"I'm beginning to understand." She examined the Greek goddess. "The detail! It's unbelievable. Even the scrollwork!"

"Could Transcontinental Communications have made a mistake? Could they have possibly printed two identical series of stocks!"

"Oh, Julien, it's not possible." She lifted her shoulders. "Well, I said that right off the top of my head. I guess it might be, but . . . oh, Julien"—she shook her short black hair—"I don't think so."

Julien leaned back against the white leather sofa. He was silent. Slowly, Kathryn turned to him. "I know what you're thinking. And that is possible. Fraud. Fraud right here in TC," she clicked the words off. "Now that is possible."

"Do you have any ideas?"

"Oh, boy, do I! Names just start hopping to the front. But I've got to be careful with my suspicions, Julien. I can't go shout 'fraud' to old so-and-so because he's stabbed me in the back a few times. Besides, Julien"—she turned to him

quizzically—"anyone I might suspect has so many other re-
courses. We're on a computer system that could be black-
mailed, we're . . . hell, just simple old-fashioned embez-
zlement would be easier than this!" she shook the certificates at him.

"Could the plate have been stolen? What about the print-
er?"

Kathryn grinned sardonically. "The obvious, of course.
But something tells me we are not dealing with the obvious."

Julien nodded.

"Julien, do you have any more of these—God forbid—
say, with the numbers 1, 2, 4, or 7 on them? I know those
are hard for a counterfeiter to duplicate."

"No, but I'd say whoever did these wouldn't have much
trouble with any number."

Kathryn fell back against the divan. She set her drink on
the table and clasped her hands together, fitting them
against her chin. "I wonder how many more there are," she
whispered.

"If you try to find out, you know what will happen."

Kathryn shuddered. "I don't have to tell you, Julien, that
in a massive corporation like TC with employees all over
the world—and many with pretty shaky loyalties—that all I
have to do is lift an eyebrow wrong and the doubt would
sweep the world before the market opens in the morning.
Panic. We start calling in every share of TC stock and it will
be sheer panic. Not only that, but we would have the FBI
and the SEC swarming over us like maggots. And that
would be the end of Transcontinental Communications."
She laughed voraciously. "If that happened, Julien, you
wouldn't even have a way to call Zurich! We own every line
to the continent."

Kathryn plunged into silence. Julien sat beside her, both contemplating the holocaust. An atom bomb dropped on Wall Street, and all that would be left would be a little mushroom cloud floating over them. And the fallout would be his reputation.

"I have a reliable investigative firm." Julien said at last. He swallowed noisily.

Kathryn turned to him slowly. Her eyes were like hard pieces of coal. Her face was tight as if she'd just risen from the grave at the sound of some horrendous bell in the distance. Suddenly, Julien knew how Kathryn Wyler had soared to the top of the business world. "I'd rather use my own." She smiled chillingly.

Should he tell her what action he'd taken? That he'd allowed some tottering old arthritic lady to go off on an antique train to the land of peublos and cave dwellers in an attempt to trace the counterfeiter who threatened to turn one of the world's most powerful corporations upside down?

"Kathryn, how much do you know about the history of this company?"

"I studied the same test cases as you did at the B school Julien." Her eyes crinkled. 'There was a family feud and one of the members was bought out, kicked off the board, and a resolution was passed that she could never own stock in the company again."

"After the company became Transcontinental Communications and went public, do you think there was someone in the company still honoring that resolution?" Julien fingered the dubious certificate.

Kathryn twisted her mouth, then glanced down at the paper Julien held. "Ah." She passed a hand theatrically over her eyes. "I think I see before me the name of Lamberton. Rings a bell. A faint, distant bell. So that's who owns that little piece of artwork. Well, I'll do some checking on my own in the morning." She rose from the divan. As she handed Julien his coat, he saw the lines deepen over the bridge of her nose.

"Julien, I have always known you to be a man of integrity. I watched you guide your clients through the 1970 crisis like the Shepherd Himself, with scarcely a nick in their portfolios. I think I can count on you. I am trusting you to keep this quiet." It was not a compliment. It was a threat.

Julien straightened his shoulders with a protective shield of arrogance. "Don't insult me, Kathryn."

"Sorry." She laughed. "In this business sometimes you have to rape the most trustworthy just to make sure they're still virgins."

He had his hand on the door and was ready to breathe a sigh of relief when she added, "But then you have to keep quiet, don't you? On the other certificate is the name of an old, reliable client of yours. Pelazoni. And if my memory is correct, since the death of her daughter, you are the sole heir. It would be funny, wouldn't it, if *her* certificate were the forgery."

Julien blushed hot. "It's not," he snapped.

"What makes you so sure?"

His thoughts whirled around inside him. Because it had nothing to do with an inheritance from Lexey Jane, he wanted to scream at her. But it did. Partly. A sharp pain shot through the ball of his right foot. He remembered his laces were still untied. Too late now. How could he get on his knee in front of Kathryn Wyler and tie his laces and explain to her it was a matter of personal integrity to prove the Mueller certificate the counterfeit? That his reputation was at stake? A reputation built on two feet doing double-time.

He could almost hear the Anderson Bridge crumbling beneath him.

It was a new kind of game for Julien. Never had he tried to mark the deck in his favor. Never had to. Until now he knew he could win because of his sheer genius. He'd prided himself on the fact that he'd never had to resort to deceit. But he'd exposed himself to Kathryn, and now his future hinged on a row of upside-down numbers, on some artful bastard who threatened to destroy him.

At the door, Kathryn smiled wickedly and said, "Julien, do come slumming again sometime."

"Kathryn, that was tacky."

Her rich laughter floated down the stairs. He shivered as the wet night air hit him.

Chapter Three

On Tuesday, March 2, at 10:45 A.M., it was still too early to go to Peaches' home, so Lexey Jane left a call for Sheila McCarthy, walked outside the hotel, blinked at the brilliant sunshine, and started across the street toward the plaza.

The plaza and the buildings framing it looked anachronistic, out of a backward time machine. Even Sears and Bell Telephone were disguised behind thick adobe structures. Lexey Jane loved it. She took a deep gulp of the fresh morning air and sat on an ornate iron bench to watch the people. She'd waited a long time for this memory trip, never losing the curiosity—why had so many of her friends made the trek out here? Runners? But her friends had stayed. Drawn to this mountainous desert as if a giant magnet lay beneath the earth, holding them to this spot. More than once, she'd used all her persuasion to get Peaches Mueller back East for a visit. "Oh, I couldn't leave my mountains," she'd say, as though they were wayward children who needed her constant surveillance and care.

Across the street, in front of Lexey Jane, was the Palace of Governors. The first government building of the territory. Along the full length of its covered portal Indians huddled against the morning chill, their blankets spread over the brick walk. And in front of each one were the inevitable clusters of Eastern tourists. They gestured with their hands, squatting to examine the silver and turquoise jewelry displayed on more blankets. From where she sat, Lexey Jane could hear the ancient, frayed question. "The first words man must have spoken," she chuckled to herself. "How much?" *Quanto?* A man held up a long necklace and the silver winked across the street at her like a daytime star.

She turned and looked at the cars moving slowly around the park set squarely in the middle of the city, and at the obelisk in the center, a memorial to all the blood shed over this quiet, sleepy town. "So this is where Edna St. Vincent Millay used to chase Witter Bynner," she mused, "around and around this very plaza." Poor dear Sefe, for Vincent had her nickname like the rest of us, came out here to marry Witter and found that no amount of chasing would ever make him like girls more than boys. She moved her lips, not hearing the sound of boots behind her.

"You're talking to yourself."

"Oh!" She jerked around. "Mannie! You startled me."

"I'm improving. At least I didn't knock you off your feet." He smiled.

She patted a spot beside her on the bench, and watched his legs crack in stiff new bluejeans as he sat beside her. "I see you've taken up the local costume."

"Well"—he stretched his long legs out in front of him—"a real estate agent showed me a couple of houses this morning. And he had bluejeans and a Coors tee-shirt

on. I decided that as a prospective client, I was a little out of
place in a suit and tie. So"—he tried smoothing out the
iron-stiff crease—"I joined the ranks."

"You've already been looking at houses this morning?
Did you find anything?"

"One had a studio. Needs a little work."

"Splendid! Are you going to buy it?"

"Mmmm." He stroked his beard. "Probably."

"You've saved your money to come to Santa Fe and be
an artist, and the very first day here you find a suitable
house. That should be cause for a little more emotion."

Mannie chuckled. "Sorry. When I get my paints and
brushes unpacked, then I'll be excited."

"You promised me last night that I'd be the first to view
the finished products of this dream of yours."

"It's still a promise."

Lexey Jane could not get over the change in Mannie
Ringer. From the stern, close-mouthed stranger at the
train station in Lamy, he had emerged phoenixlike into a
cheerful, talkative friend. One who made concerned, late-
night calls . . .

"What were you talking to yourself about when I walked
up?"

Lexey Jane laughed. "Old friends. I knew a lot of people
who moved out here in the twenties and thirties—when it
was the thing to do." She suddenly caught herself. "Not
that it still isn't the ideal place for artists. I knew Sven Gus-
tafson, Greta Garbo's brother. She used to visit him out
here and I've been trying to imagine her slouching about
the plaza in her big floppy hats and slacks. And during his
Kon Tiki days, Thor Heyerdahl used to spend quite a bit of
time here. Strange, don't you think? A man of the sea
drawn to this desert. And Lily Pons and André Kostelanetz

used to live near the opera house. Vera Zorina and Greer Garson still live here, and . . . " she paused. " . . . and John Ehrlichman. I guess that inventory says something about our new definition of fame. I guess it's infamy that succeeds these days." She turned to Mannie. A shadow crossed his face. The color drained from it. What had she said to make the scars on his forehead stand out like dark slashes? He was suddenly that stranger at the train station, collapsed into some morbid brooding.

"In fact," she went on quickly. "I'm having lunch with one of those friends today. Peaches. Peaches Mueller. Wanted to be a weaver. And weaving . . . well, it just wasn't the thing to do if you were the daughter of a millionaire from Wilmington, Delaware. So Peaches moved to Santa Fe and we all thought she'd toppled off the face of the earth."

"Still weaving?"

Lexey Jane sighed with relief at the crack in Mannie's dark silence. "I don't know. Probably. She was quite good at it. Extraordinarily good."

"I understand that kind of dedication. Leaving your roots to follow a dream," Mannie said quietly.

"Yes. Yes, I'm sure you do." For the first time she noticed his hands. It had been too dark in the bar last night, but now in the sunlight the long, tapered, strong fingers lay on the thighs of his new bluejeans.

"Mannie, your hands are beautiful!"

Mannie grinned shyly and lifted one of them in the air.

Lexey Jane reached out, grabbed his wrist and looked at his watch. "Is that what time it is? Oh dear, Shiela will be wondering where I am."

"No, she won't." Mannie was standing and waving. "There she is. Over there by the curb."

Lexey Jane saw the tiny Irish face light up as she waved to them from the station wagon. This morning she was enveloped in an enormous striped poncho. Beneath it peeked a pair of bluejeans, undoubtedly naval surplus from the battle of Dunkirk.

"Just coming over to get you," she called brightly.

Mannie was already on the other side, opening the door for Lexey Jane. "Say, Mannie, if you'll stand in the shower in those jeans they'll shape up," Shiela giggled. Lexey Jane darted a glance at the girl, then at the bearded man who kept assaulting her with his moods. How long had that ride been last night from Lamy to Santa Fe?

Lexey Jane took Mannie's hand and worked herself into the front seat. "That's a handsome watch," she whispered.

"Thank you. Swiss."

"Yes, I know." She smiled. And was immediately sorry. The creases in Mannie's forehead turned abruptly to scars. He was still scowling at her as Shiela drove off.

The watch was a Bucherer manual digital, the only watch the Swiss didn't export. You had to be in Switzerland, or on the Continent at least, to buy one. But what does that mean? Good Lord, Lexey Jane, what's wrong with someone buying a watch in Europe? You've done so yourself several times. And you're not guilty of anything. After all, it could have been a gift. Now just stop it.

"Better tell me where you're going," Shiela was saying.

"Oh, yes, I guess I should." She blinked at the tiny bright girl. "Hyde Park. Here." She pulled Peaches' letter from her purse. Her friend had drawn a beautiful map, even shading in the trees and miniature adobes she'd drawn as reference points, delicately crisscrossing at the corners to give them depth and dimension.

"This isn't a map. This is a work of art," Shiela exclaimed, taking it from her. She wheeled around the plaza, glanced at the map, then at the street. "If everyone could draw a map like this, nobody would ever be lost again," she chuckled.

"Have you known Mannie Ringer long?"

Shiela's head jerked around. The small black eyes narrowed. "That's a funny question. I could ask you the same thing, you know." The whispery voice was angry. The small, booted foot pressed down hard on the accelerator.

"Then ask me," Lexey Jane retorted. She was not accustomed to having her hand slapped.

"All right, I will. How long have you known Mannie Ringer?"

"Since last night. We came on the same train. I had a drink in the bar with him after, I presume, you delivered him," Lexey Jane snapped back. She saw the poncho slump on Shiela's shoulders.

"Didn't mean to make you angry. I drove him in from Lamy. He was nice and friendly, so it didn't take long to be on a first-name basis."

Lexey Jane studied the girl's profile as the sunlight flickered across it. By sheer instinct she knew that Shiela McCarthy was protecting something. An ache. An ache that strangled in the whispery voice. An ache so deep that if the cold air hit it, it would throw the small bundled girl to her knees. And Lexey Jane was not sure Shiela McCarthy would be able to get up again.

She suddenly felt herself jerked back against the seat. The station wagon was climbing straight up! In the distance, she could see the snow-capped peaks of the Sangre de Cristo mountains rising up to the sky. "With all due respects to Sir Edmund Hilary, I hope Peaches doesn't live up there," she thought. She couldn't speak. The ascent pressed against her lungs. Her chest buckled as Shiela, with a grinding shift of gears, rushed onto a dirt road. A jogger bobbed up in front of them. Lexey Jane blinked at the whirr of sweatshirt and tennis shoes that flashed in the corner of her eye. Her nails dug into the seat as the car rose and dipped, swaying against the cliff on their left, bouncing perilously near the chasm on their right. Scrub pine rose up in front of her, ran past her in a streaking blur. Chamisa bushes rattled against the car like scraggly monsters. She risked a timorous glance out the window and flinched at the rushing air outside the door. She grasped her cane furiously. No one had the right to take chances with her life like this! Just as the girl's name throttled in her throat, Shiela whirled in front of a long adobe house. The tires slid in a massive, grinding halt.

"What time do you want me to pick you up?" the girl asked tightly.

Lexey Jane bristled. "I'll call you." Her knees trembling, she climbed slowly from the car and clutched her cane.

"She's expecting me," Lexey Jane added with the same terseness. She waited until Shiela was a swirl of dust disappearing down the road before she turned and knocked on the carved wooden door. Grumbling under her breath at the impudence of youth, she waited for Peaches. Silence. She knocked again, pressing her ear against the door, listening for sounds inside the house. A strange, long-necked bird scurried through the brush, startling her.

"Peaches? Peaches! It's Lexey Jane."

For one uncomprehending moment, she turned back to the cloud of dust in the distance. A frantic urge siezed her to hail the girl back, as if something waited inside that house she did not want to confront alone. A faint rumbling reached her ears. She looked around, then up. High, high above her, against the dazzling blue sky, a silent jet unfurled a long white ribbon. She watched it until a breeze whispered through the pine trees close to the house, bringing her back. "Nonsense," she scolded herself. She called again. "Peaches! It's Duzey!"

Silence again. She looked around at the desolate landscape. "It's just unfamiliar, that's all," she spoke aloud.

There was a large window on the front. She tried to peer through it, but it was covered with a heavy woven fabric, undoubtedly a Peaches Mueller product. She rapped loudly on the glass with her cane. She tried the door. Locked.

"Well, Mrs. Sherlock Holmes, it is obvious that Peaches has lost her hearing," she grumbled as she started around the side of the house. She staggered through rock and gravel that rolled under her feet. A low bush maliciously tore at her leg, and she struck at it with her cane. At the back was a small porch and another door. It was unlocked.

"Peaches?"

The door opened into a kitchen. She went through another door into a large hallway. Brilliant sunlight streamed through a skylight and bounced off the white walls. It blinded her. She blinked, then squinted. The polished wooden floors were covered in thick woven rugs. Colorful tapestries hung along an alcove. Well, she certainly had the right house. Her cane sunk silently into a carpet, and it occurred to her that when she did find Peaches— who was probably in the bathroom or asleep—she just might scare the be-Jesus out of her.

Through a small doorway something caught her eye. An enormous wooden machine with great long wooden poles and boards, shafts and dowels, shuttles and heddles filled the room beyond.

Of course, the loom. Peaches' loom. She ducked her

head around the corner. Empty, except for a new rug on the loom with a shaft of wool stuck neatly between the warp threads.

She crossed the hall and walked through a wide archway into the living room. "Ah, Peaches. There you are. I've been pounding on the door . . ."

The plump woman sat in a chair before the fireplace, near the window on which Lexey Jane had rapped her cane. Sitting quite properly in an Edwardian armchair, her hands folded neatly in her lap, Peaches Mueller stared straight at Lexey Jane with quite dry, quite dead eyes.

She braced herself on the cane. A moan was still circling the room, bouncing off the white walls. It took a moment for Lexey Jane to realize it had come from her. When she opened them, she instinctively reached out to straighten the curled gray hair that stood mussed on the side. Quickly, she drew back her hand. "Don't touch the . . . the . . . " Oh, how could she say it? Corpse? Body? "Don't touch Peaches," she corrected herself with agony. She glanced at the fireplace. The charcoal was cold. On a table, within Peaches' reach, was an atomizer for emphysema, a vial of oxygen for asthma and a telephone.

Resolutely, she dialed the number pasted on the front of the phone. "I want to report a murder," she said firmly. She looked from the small table to Peaches. "She must have talked to me from this very chair," she thought. "And then called the man who had given her the stock certificate," she groaned aloud. "Oh, Peaches! Why did you let me tell you?"

She walked in circles around the room to fill the silence of the staring eyes. But they kept following her. "In the movies someone always reaches over and closes them."

The stillness was suffocating. The tapestries, the carpets

muffled her very breathing. Instantly, in a motion that fluttered a wall hanging, Lexey Jane whirled angrily, planted herself in front of the dead woman, and looked straight at her. "I'll find out who did this, dear. Don't worry."

Then, Lexey Jane cocked her head and examined the face, the plump cheeks now sunken a bit and ashen with death. Lexey Jane nodded reassuringly. "You look quite good, Peaches. For sixty-nine, you look remarkable."

At the sound of wheels on the gravel outside, she tottered quickly toward the front door, started to open it, but suddenly pulled up her skirt and wrapped it around the knob. When she opened the door, the tall, thickset man was staring at a wide band of lace above two knobby knees. She looked up at the mustached face, the black eyes shaded by a cowboy hat, and drew back in dismay. Oh dear, they've sent Pancho Villa!

"Excuse the indecent exposure, officer, but I didn't want to erase any fingerprints." She dropped her skirt.

"Someone called and said there was a murder out here," the mustached man said and looked at her skeptically. Outside, another officer was climbing from the car. Short and rotund, he hitched up his holster, but it fell immediately back into place below his belly.

"I was that someone officer. Yes. There has been a murder. Peaches Mueller. My good friend." She had the odd feeling she was making an introduction.

The officer took a hesitant step forward, decided against it, and planted both feet firmly in the open doorway. "You live around here, lady?" He glanced askance at her.

"Pelazoni. Lexey Jane Pelazoni. And no, I don't live around here. I live in Wilmington, Delaware, and I came to Santa Fe yesterday to see Mrs. Mueller. Who is in the living room. Dead."

"You're the lady who called." She nodded. "Anyone else in the house?"

"Oh!" How stupid. Holmes would have searched the premises immediately. "I certainly hope not," she answered.

He called over his shoulder. "Hey, Joe!"

The short, fat officer appeared around the corner in his sunglasses, and Pancho Villa rolled his black eyes in Lexey Jane's direction as if to say, "Another crazy one. Keep your eyes on her."

They both walked past her, their boots clattering on the polished floor. "Now, lady, if you'll just show us . . . " The senior officer stopped. He had turned the corner at that moment and saw Peaches sitting decorously in her chair. He crossed the room and grabbed her wrist in his hand, checking the pulse.

How odd, Lexey Jane thought, watching him, that I knew she was dead, that it never occurred to me to check her pulse.

The thick mustache turned to her. "Lady, she's dead all right." His eyes scanned the room. "Now what makes you think she's been murdered? Looks like a natural death to me." There was a faint smirk beneath the mustache. "Did she have any illness . . . uh . . . ailments you know of?" Officiously, he pulled a pad and pen from his pocket.

"Because I. . . ." I can't tell him why I'm here! She shuddered. Do I tell him that a cranky old arthritic woman is tracking a brilliant counterfeiter who gave my old Vassar roommate forged stock in return for a million dollars because Peaches wanted vengeance for an old family feud and the whole affair is threatening to botch up one of the world's largest corporations? She glanced slyly up at the thick black mustache, and shook her head. This officer thinks I've already watched too much television. "She had asthma . . . and a touch of emphysema," she answered haltingly, "but still . . ."

"Oh, well." He motioned toward the fireplace. "See that?" He pointed to the charcoal. "That just ain't safe to burn in a closed-up room like this. Puts off fumes that'll knock you out everytime." He swelled to full height with this bit of knowledge.

"But she looks so . . . so *arranged*," Lexey Jane protested. "If she'd had a coughing spasm, her hands would have been different. They would not have been folded neatly in her lap!"

"Probably fell asleep," the officer mumbled.

Lexey Jane bristled at the solicitous tone of voice.

"Did she live alone?" He was writing something on his pad.

"Yes."

"Did she have any friends here in Santa Fe? Any family? Anybody we can contact?"

In the corner of her eye, Lexey Jane could see the open address book on a desk next to the wall. Somehow she had to get it without . . . "What is your name?" she demanded.

"Montoya. Captain Bennie Montoya." The mustache looked up suddenly. "And you say she had emph . . . emphysema," spelling it out laboriously. "Any friends?" he repeated.

"No family living. I don't know about friends. I'm sure she had many. I'll inquire around." Slowly, she inched toward the desk. She was close enough to see it open to . . . to her name. Pelazoni.

"And the name of the deceased?"

"Marybelle Peaches Lamberton Mueller." She waited for

him to glance disbelievingly at her before she moved. But Bennie Montoya kept on writing. "M-u-e-l-l-e-r," Lexey Jane spelled it for him. Her hand shot out behind her and grabbed the book. It was in her purse.

"Hey Bennie!" The short officer came through the door, blinking in the sun. "There's some funny-looking holes in the ground at the side of the house."

"That was my cane, you idiot!" Lexey Jane snapped. "The front door was locked and I had to come in the back way."

Bennie and Joe exchanged a shrug of shoulders. "Better call Sanchez and have him send somebody out here for the body," Bennie said.

"What about an autopsy and a coronor's report, and all those things?" Lexey Jane asked, her head tilted back like an expert, "and photographs. We ought to take photographs of . . ."

"Look lady." Captain Bennie Montoya soared above her. She could see his eyes above the mustache.

"Lexey Jane. Lexey Jane Pelazoni," she interrupted tersely.

"Yeah, Mrs. Peltzioni. Look, we got thousands of these old people who retire out here, live alone, and once a week we find one of 'em dead in their homes. Now if we thought they'd all been murdered we wouldn't have time to do anything else, would we?"

"The name is Pelazoni. And I will pay for an autopsy."

Bennie Montoya rolled his eyes at the ceiling and let out an explosion of air. "Jesus!" His head came down. "Joe, tell 'em this lady, this Mrs. Peltzioni, wants an autopsy done on the body. Says she'll pay for it. Now." He looked back at Lexey Jane. From long habit Bennie Montoya licked the ballpoint pen as though it were a pencil. It left a blue line on the tip of his tongue. "Where you staying?"

"The La Fonda. Room 240."

He wrote it down, slapped the small spiral pad shut, and stuck it in his pocket. "Now I'm going to take you back there, and you stay there, okay? We might want to get in touch with you." He lowered his head commandingly.

Lexey Jane bit the inside of her cheek. She must remember to tell that young hippie, if she ever saw him again, that there are certain disadvantages to being old.

"Who's that?"

Bennie Montoya was looking over her head at something in the doorway. Lexey Jane turned to follow his eyes. The face was invisible. As white as the wall it leaned against, the eyes stared above an oversized poncho. "Shelia!" Strange, none of them had heard her drive up. Why was she here? Why had she come back?

"Shiela?"

There was something wrong with the girl. She held onto the wall. Her mouth was clamped shut, but Lexey Jane felt the girl had screamed—a haunting, primal, gutted scream of terror. Some protective instinct rushed Lexey Jane across the room. She grabbed the thick poncho at the shoulders. "Shiela! Did you know her?"

"She's dead."

"Did you know her?" Bennie Montoya was beside her, pad in hand, diligently licking the tip of the ballpoint.

"I . . . no . . . yes. I took some weaving lessons from her." Slowly, the poncho and bluejeans resumed a human shape. Shiela brushed a hand across her eyes. Bennie Montoya was asking her name.

"Shiela McCarthy. I drive the wagon for the La Fonda. I came back to see if Mrs. Pelazoni needed a ride back to town. We had an argument on the way out here, and I wanted to . . ."

"Address?"

"Uh . . .1300 Canyon Road." She looked frantically from Lexey Jane to Bennie Montoya. "Why are you asking me all these questions?" She was herself again.

"Because she may have been murdered," Lexey Jane answered, watching the girl carefully.

"Murdered!" The response seemed genuine. But then, if physics professors are plumbers . . .

Bennie Montoya threw her a disgusted look. "Routine," he mumbled. "You going to take her back to the hotel?"

"Yes. Yes, of course."

Lexey Jane allowed Bennie Montoya to help her to the station wagon. Behave yourself, she kept cautioning her tongue. Cooperate with the authorities. That's what Julien would tell you.

"You'll probably have to sign some papers and stuff like that," Bennie said as he opened the door for her.

"Of course," Lexey Jane cooed unctuously. "Anything I can do to help."

On Tuesday, March 2, promptly at four P.M., Mannie Ringer turned a key in a lock on Palace Avenue. He was excited, smiling to himself. The lock gave a possessive click, the door opened, and a rush of stale air met him—the odor of dust and damp clay. Grunting a little as he picked up his suitcase, he walked through the small kitchen and into a room sagging onto the back of the house. Chuckling, he looked out the large north window, then around the room at a paint-splattered bench and an old chair with three legs and bricks where the fourth had been. Then he opened a closet and deposited the suitcase. It hit the floor with a loud clank.

"Thank you, Iris!" he exclaimed.

From there he hurried to Brenner's where he purchased

canvas and stretchers and a wooden palette. He grabbed tubes of pigment, oils and acrylics, tested the fine mink-hair brushes on his tongue. He found a heavy wooden easel that adjusted to his height, and at the last minute gathered up a fistful of charcoal and two enormous sketch pads.

"You going into the business?" The clerk smiled.

"You bet," Mannie replied jubilantly. "I've waited a life-time for this. I am an artist."

One thin eyebrow rose sardonically. "Oh? I never would have known."

While the clerk added his bill, Mannie took some tens and twenties from his pocket. Carefully, he laid them on the counter. He ran the edge of his palm along the bills to flatten them. His finger traced the penurious face of Andrew Jackson. Instinctively, he turned them over and examined the backs.

The clerk glanced up from his pad. "What's wrong?"

Mannie chewed his lip. "Uh . . . over at the grocery store, checker said counterfeits were running around. Thought I'd better look at these." He laughed.

At 4:17 P.M. on Tuesday, March 2, Lexey Jane closed the door of her room and leaned back against it for a long moment. The ride into town with Shiela McCarthy had been a deadly, taut silence. Twice Lexey Jane had risked a glance at the petite face. The color had come back to the cheeks, but they were still pale. "When did you take weaving lessons from Peaches?" she'd asked.

"Can't talk about it now." The answer sounded as hollow as an open grave.

When she had let Lexey Jane off at the hotel, she'd smiled. But it was as if someone had pulled a string and quickly let go.

Now, in her room, Lexey Jane anxiously reached in her purse for Peaches' address book and flipped it open. "Oh!" she moaned, sitting on the bed. The book was filled with years and years of names, names written over names, telephone numbers scratched and rewritten in smudged margins. "I'd have better luck with the telephone book," she grumbled.

Suddenly, a small slip of paper fluttered to the floor. Excited, Lexey Jane leaned forward to pick it up. "Ah!" The pain jabbed along her spine, into her hip socket. Taking a deep breath, she tried again. Slowly, gingerly, her fingers found the paper on the floor and closed around it and she straightened with a loud sigh.

There were four names: Ivy Boydon, Jerry Kirwen, Iris, and the initials R.H. "Jerry. Jerry. The hippie's name was Jerry. Surely, you don't suppose . . . ?" Quickly, she looked in the phone book. Kirk, Kirkpatrick, Kirschke, Kisler. No Kirwen listed. "Damn," she exclaimed. She found Ivy Boydon, wrote down the number and address. R.H. What or who did that stand for? And Iris. Who is Iris?

The phone screamed at her elbow. She jumped, and the mattress bounced and rolled beneath her. "Hello?"

"You must have had a good lunch. I've called twice," Julien puffed on the other end.

"Oh, Julien, it wasn't nice at all." Tears rolled down her cheeks. "Peaches is dead."

"What?"

"She's dead, Julien." Trembling, she wiped her face.

"Oh, Lexey Jane, I'm sorry . . . sorry that . . ."

"Well, at my age, death becomes a way of life. Still . . . " she held her lips tight to keep them from shaking. "She looked so helpless."

"Did you get to talk to her at all?"

"I'm afraid not, Julien. She was dead when I got there."

A heavy, retreating sigh came from the other end. "I guess our problem has been solved for us." His voice shifted. "Now there's a flight straight from Albuquerque in the morning. I'll meet you at . . ."

"Oh, Julien, I can't leave! Peaches was murdered."

She listened carefully to the long silence. The voice came slow, "Now, Lexey Jane . . ."

"I'm sure of it, Julien."

"If you're right, then let the authorities take care of it."

"But they won't. They don't believe me. I've got to stay Julien. I may have murdered her myself."

"What are you saying?"

"I did talk to her last night. And . . . oh, Julien," her voice kept rising beyond her control. "Peaches got it out of me—that the stock was counterfeit. And . . . and I'm afraid she called the man who gave her the certificate . . . Julien?" She glanced fearfully at the list of names in her hand. "Was it a man?" Did little Irish lasses and sometime-authors commit murder? "Did Peaches ever say?"

"No. I only advised her strongly against the transaction. It depleted her resources."

"I know you didn't like her, Julien, but you don't have to sound nasty about it."

"Lexey Jane!" She heard a unique exasperation in Julien's voice. "I don't think you understand the consequences of this whole thing."

"Of course, I do. But it's not the end of the world, you know."

"It may be the end of mine." She could hear him puffing like a train straining to climb a mountain. "I was wrong in letting you go down there. I want you on that plane in the morning. There's nothing more you can do."

"Sorry, Julien. I'm staying for the funeral. By the way, how are you coming on that end?"

"I'm waiting for a phone call right now. As soon as I know anything I'll call you back." His voice was flat with resignation.

The moment she hung up, she realized she'd forgotten to ask about Peaches' will.

Suddenly, there was a knock on the door and Shiela McCarthy stuck her head in. "Mrs. Pelazoni! You must lock your door! There are all kinds of nuts running around."

"Afraid of fire," Lexey Jane snapped. She didn't like revealing her eccentricities to just anybody, even if they were Ph.D., M.A., author and chauffeur.

"There are a lot worse things than fire," Shiela whispered. She jerked her poncho around her. "I got paid today and I wondered, well, I wondered if I could show you some of Santa Fe tomorrow. It's my day off."

"When do the books get written?" Lexey Jane made certain her smile was gentle. After all, the girl was making some sort of peace offering.

"At stoplights and checkout lines." Shiela grinned. "I'd really like to give you a tour and take you to lunch. You seem to like history as much as I do."

"Fine."

"Then, eleven o'clock tomorrow. Okay?"

"Okay."

But ten minutes later Lexey Jane frowned and clucked her tongue. The jogger Shiela had passed on the mountain road flicked past her memory. Even Peaches with her asthma had strolled the back paths as if she had Peruvian lungs. Everyone in Santa Fe walked or rode bicycles or owned a sweatsuit. What a neat way to discard somebody. Drive up to the edge of a chasm, open the door, and push her out. TOURIST TOPPLES DURING STROLL. Well, she would take all the precautions. Lock her door, ram her cane against it. There are ways—she smiled—even if you are an old reject.

The moment Julien hung up, the phone rang beneath his hand.

"Is this the lawyer who stubbed his toe?"

Julien winced as his right foot suddenly cramped. "Kathryn, I've just had some bad news so I'm not in the mood for jokes."

"Oh? My mother always told me, if you've got one foot stuck in a hole, you sure don't want it to snow."

She waited for a laugh, but Julien was taking off his shoe, trying to massage his bent toes.

"Julien?"

"Yes."

"Get ready for the snow." She heard a dismal blast of air into the receiver. "The plates are in a vault in a strong room. Tighter 'n a tick, as we say down South. There are only two. One was discontinued in 1952. The other has been used since. Now, as a safeguard, whoever gets in that vault has to sign away his life. *If* someone borrowed the plate, and *if* he signed his name, there's no record in the computer." Kathryn took a deep breath. "I checked with the little man who does the printing. The last issue was in 1970, and he keeps an accurate record against ours. He's been doing it, or overseeing it, for TC since 1949. So it's a little hard to line him up as a suspect. No children to put through school, no expensive wife, no greedy blackmailing mistress—none of your juicy motives."

"And fraud?" he asked hopefully.

"Oh, yes, then there's fraud," she answered brightly.

"That's going to take some fancy footwork, Julien, and I don't want to play the highpowered cat-and-mouse game just yet. Not only is it costly, but I don't want to set a brouhaha into motion if all we have is some half-assed engraver working after hours."

"He may have only half an ass, but there's one thing he doesn't lack."

"What's that?"

"Talent."

"Don't remind me, Julien."

"Were you able to check on the Lamberton family?"

"What's left of them. It was scanty pickings. Your Mrs. Mueller is the only one still living who was on the original board. Brother's dead. Aunts, uncles, cousins either dead or scattered. I even got as far down as second cousins, but only one owns any TC stock . . . not enough to control anything . . . to force anyone to honor a stupid resolution, unless he's got some friend inside the corporation I don't know about. Name's Rudolph Hiatt, second cousin, last address was Bordeaux, France. But for the last two years his dividends have gone straight into an account at the Chemical Bank here in New York. Uh . . . what about Mrs. Mueller? Does she suspect anything?"

Julien rolled a pencil back and forth across his desk. "She's dead."

"Oh, that's nice. If you can't take the stocks out of circulation, you remove the client."

"I don't suspect foul play." Julien made a silent apology to Lexey Jane. "She was sixty-nine and asthmatic."

"Julien, I was making a bad joke, and you jumped. Do you think she was murdered?"

"No, no. Of course not," he answered with all the certainty he could muster.

"There are heirs, I suppose?" Kathryn's voice cracked like ice splinters.

"One."

"Well, if nothing else rolls up the carpet, that will. Just try to keep him from liquidating. Okay?"

"I haven't met him, but I'll try."

"For the moment that takes care of 99999. The problem is, Julien, how many more certificates are there like that? We've got 94, almost 95, *million* outstanding shares between 237,000 stockholders. And how do I know who's got the real thing and who's got the forgeries? It's a mess!"

Julien turned in his chair and looked out the window. Down below him workers were fixing the sewer. They'd blocked off the street and he could see the orange flag waving traffic into a turnaround. "It's more like a dead end," he answered.

Kathryn Wyler tapped a Camel irritably on her desk. The lights on the intercom at her side were blinking like frantic little imps, but she ignored them.

She had lied to Julien. But it had been necessary to protect her "secret service" system. The cat-and-mouse game was not all that expensive. On the contrary. Already, for the mere sum of $525 she had unearthed some startling information. The moment Julien had left her apartment last night, she had set it into motion. Save The Garbage. The clarion call came from an old computer term *gigo:* garbage in, garbage out. Every cleaning maid, every maintenance man had been alerted. "The cloth and broom force," Kathryn smiled. All those wastebaskets being emptied, desks straightened, all those brooms sweeping behind hidden corners. She ticked off the results:

So far she'd found out that IBM was planning to buy a

small company with a patent pending for a new type of computer. She would have to investigate that, see if TC should buy it out from under them.

There was discontent within the top ranks of Sellers Limited. The chairman of the board was having an affair with the treasurer's wife.

A crumpled memo told her that Watson at North American Transportation was being boosted for a big promotion. That was nice, since he was a personal friend.

TWA was working on a merger with Delta.

And Zorini Lines was perfecting a telstar credit card system to eliminate the volumes of paperwork in shipping. That had infinite possibilities for TC, she mused.

But so far no clues of fraud inside the company.

All this information should have made her day rather pleasant. But she lit the cigarette and smoked it with disgust. Being privy to trash had contributed to the meteoric ascent of Kathryn Wyler, the fairhaired genius of TC. Well, you could hardly say "fairhaired," she chuckled, smoothing her thick black crop.

She thought of Julien Strauss working on summit levels while he gathered his *real* information from the subterranean world of secretaries, filing clerks, messengers. Their methods were similar; they simply worked on different levels. Sometimes crossing in the aisles, intercepting one another. Yet nothing, *nothing* had turned up that would throw any light on that damned forgery!

She glanced down at the note about Zorini Shipping Lines, trying to eliminate the infinite carbon copies of international trade. "I always said we'd drown in a sea of paper," she grumbled at one of the flashing lights on the intercom. It's just that Kathryn Wyler never had any premonitions of going down with the ship.

Chapter Four

"Gin. No ice."

The young waitress blanched at the old lady who had shriveled in the chair. "Wow!" she whispered. In a moment she returned, setting the glass on a napkin. "That's pretty heavy." The old lady looked up at her, bewildered. "Warm gin," the waitress explained. "That's pretty heavy."

Lexey Jane smiled wanly, raised the glass to the empty chair opposite her. "Forgive me, Peaches," she said softly.

After two gins, the arthritic pain was easing a little. She sighed and leaned back. At the same moment something clutched her shoulder and squeezed it hard. She bit her lip to keep from screaming. A hand was wrapped around her bones, grinding them together. Sawtooth pain jagged up her neck, down through her arm.

"Thought I'd find you here."

The hand released its grip, and Lexey Jane gulped a deep breath. "Mannie! You frightened me."

"Frightened you? What . . . ?" The bearded man folded his long body into a chair nearest her. "Hey, did I hurt you? I forget how strong I am sometimes." He reached over and patted her arm gently. "I'm sorry."

"It's all right. I've just had so much cortisone, I'm afraid my bones are like lacework."

Mannie leaned back and shoved his hand deep into his pocket. He laid a ring of keys on the table. "You are looking at the proud owner of a four-room adobe hacienda." He laughed.

"Oh, Mannie. Splendid. And it has a studio?"

"Sort of. It's hanging onto the back of the house. And I do mean hanging. But I'll jack it up. I'm good with my hands."

"Yes, I imagine you are." Lexey Jane felt the pain in her shoulder slowly run its course.

"Hey, you don't look too chipper. Something wrong?"

Lexey Jane looked out across the darkened room filled with people huddled at tables. A combo was playing at the far end. The music was too loud, too cacophonic—like the pain inside her. "I'm sitting here hoping that someone will understand why I'm having her hacked to pieces."

Mannie looked at her, chewing his lip. His beard moved from side to side. "That will take a little explanation."

"The friend I was to meet for lunch today? She was dead when I got there." Her voice was leaden. "And I asked for an autopsy." She shuddered. "You know what that means." Tears stung her eyes. "We were girls together. I keep seeing Peaches as she was then, all pink and healthy. She had full cheeks—Ann Miller cheeks—that pressed up against her eyes." She broke off.

Mannie's head jerked so visibly his beard trembled. The two o'clock in the morning phone call. *She got herself killed.* Someone had been watching them that night in the bar. Iris? No, he felt a twinge of relief, someone had been watching Lexey Jane. Don't think about cause and effect, Mannie, he told himself. It always makes you give yourself away.

"Hey now." Mannie leaned toward her. "You know what I read someplace? That we're made up of all these little molecules of energy just spinning around, and when we die that same energy just keeps on spinning—only in different places, different shapes. You know, not altogether in a human form. So it really doesn't matter about your friend, you see. The autopsy, I mean. All her molecules are still spinning around somewhere."

Lexey Jane smiled at his efforts.

At that moment, the waitress set a drink in front of Mannie and he pulled some bills from his pocket.

"You want another one of those?" The waitress wrinkled her nose at Lexey Jane's empty glass.

"Think so."

Mannie turned his drink around in his hand. "You remember those two men the other night, standing in the doorway? The hippie blond-looking old guy and the other one?" he blurted. "Have you ever seen them before?"

Absently, Lexey Jane answered, "The other one looked familiar. I've seen his face before. I think it was in a book. Probably looked like someone else."

Suddenly, Mannie spread the bills out on the table. "Hey," he said brightly, "there are bogus tens and twenties going around town. And I think I got passed a ten." He glanced at her to see if this new subject was enough distraction. Mannie saw two small eyes glittering at him with unusual interest. He drew back involuntarily. Now you've done it, he thought grimly. With that dumb-assed question

about the two men. Cause and effect. It will be your down-
fall, Mannie Ringer.

"How can you tell?"

"Pretty easy nowadays," Mannie answered tightly.

Lexey Jane watched him closely. Was it reluctance in his
voice? She must be careful. More nonchalant. "Show me,"
she sighed.

"Well, if you'll look at this ten, you'll see the front is dull
and sort of flat. Don't know if you can tell in this light. But
look here. Look at old Hamilton's hairline. Detail's sloppy.
The fine lines are missing. And the seal—see, those little
sawtooth points are uneven. A couple are even broken off
right here. Now look at the back." He turned it over.
"Counterfeiters rarely pay attention to the back of a bill."

Lexey Jane examined it in the dim light. It did look a little
smeared.

Mannie clucked his tongue regretfully. "Lot of awful-
looking junk around nowadays, what with printing machines and photo-offset processes. Used to be a time when
a counterfeiter spent months hand-engraving a steel plate,
even making his own paper. They were artists, really. Just
as good as Rembrandt or Renoir or any of the old masters.
But"—he shrugged—"they never got any recognition for
it."

Lexey Jane studied him. His voice was light and chattery,
but she detected a certain forlornness, as if Mannie himself
had just lost a dear friend. Suddenly he chuckled, amused
at some memory. "There was one counterfeiter who got it.
Recognition, I mean," he went on, "Jim the Penman they
called him. He used to say that the bills he turned out at
home were better than what the Federal government printed. And he was right. After he went to prison, collectors
paid $100 for copies of his hand-drawn $50 bills, and as
much as $250 for his $100 bills." Mannie sighed and sipped

his drink thoughtfully. "He was a true artist. The Secret Service gave him a pretty prominent place in that museum of theirs up in Washington."

"Maybe we should use something besides paper." Lead him along slowly.

"Hell, paper money has been floating around since the fourteenth century in China. Besides, I'm glad I didn't have to pay for that house today with cockleshells." He grinned.

"How do you know all this?" Lexey Jane kept her laugh easy and light.

Mannie Ringer jerked his head up from the bills spread over the table. His face was flushed. "I . . . I used to work on the third floor of the Federal Reserve building in New York," he answered slowly.

"What's so special about the third floor?"

"That's . . . that's where the counterfeit detectors work. They sort and count the currency coming in from banks in the area . . ."

Lexey Jane tried to look bored, but she couldn't. The warm gin had destroyed her caution. How could she remain bland when his words raised a hue and cry inside her? She listened, not just to his voice, but to all of him. He was manufacturing the story! He was fabricating it, carefully engraving it in the air for her. She struggled to keep from blurting out, who the hell are you, Mannie Ringer?

Just at the moment when she thought she could no longer keep that question inside her, a figure darted behind one of the thick pillars in the lobby. She jerked around, squinting through the irregular windows that separated the bar from the rest of the hotel. Pale hair. A glimpse of a lean, youthful figure. Tennis shoes and sweatshirt. She half-rose from her chair. Jerry?

"Excuse me a moment, Mannie. I think there's someone

I know in the lobby." She stood, tottering a moment, waiting to gain certainty with the cane. She walked to the pillar and peered around it. A wrinkled face like a crumpled brown paper bag peered back at her. A hand reached up and straightened long black braids over a shoulder blanket. "One dollar if you take my picture," the face said.

"Inflation is everywhere." She scanned the lobby. I saw him dart behind this pillar. There was no way for him to leave without being seen! She walked back into the bar. The chairs at her table were empty.

Ever since he'd been promoted to head of the homicide division ("division" consisting of himself, Joe Archuleta, and a secretary), Bennie Montoya had allowed himself the luxury of Tecate beer. He grabbed one now from the refrigerator, opened it, smeared fresh lime around the sharp triangle, and sprinkled salt over the top. He took a long gulp, leaning back and letting the icy cold slide down his throat. "Ahhhhh." In rapid sequence came a series of belches. He sat down on the divan and spread both legs out on the coffee table. With one toe, he tried to work off the left boot. His heel stuck halfway up. Without moving from his splayed position, he tried the boot on his right foot. No luck. Belching once more, he laid his head back and closed his eyes.

At that moment, the phone jangled. One eye opened, then the other. He took another sip of beer, then wiped his mustache with the back of his hand. At last he got up, stumbling in the half-on, half-off boots. "Yeah?"

"Hey, Bennie, we got something that, well . . . it's weird."

"Just tell me, Joe. Skip the analysis."

"This garbage man called a little while ago, and he found a leg at the city dump."

"A what?"

"A leg . . . you know, a leg. A human leg. Like you walk on."

"Jesus!" Bennie Montoya slammed the can down so hard the beer spurted up like a geyser.

"I sent two guys out there already . . . " Joe added.

"Get the bulldozer," Bennie sighed. "I'll pick you up."

On Tuesday, March 2, at 6:37 P.M., Bennie Montoya and Joe Archuleta sat in the patrol car watching the bulldozer attack the Santa Fe dump. In the next thirty minutes the machine unearthed seven car batteries, one maple rocker—Sears Roebuck vintage—a mountain of tin cans, and an avalanche of green plastic bags.

"Jesus." Bennie fumbled in his pocket for cigarettes.

"When I was a kid I thought this was the best place in town," Joe said. "I'd come out here and go through the piles right after they dumped 'em. Got to know everbody's garbage in town." He grinned. "You know you can tell a lot about a person just from his garbage."

Bennie exhaled a long, straight line of smoke.

"My wife says you can tell a lot about a person just from looking in their medicine cabinet," Joe went on. "Everytime we go anywhere, she goes and prowls through the medicine cabinet."

Bennie blinked. He'd picked up crabs last month and the oil and powder were still in his medicine cabinet. He'd have to remember not to invite Joe and his wife over until he'd cleaned house.

"What about the hospital?" Joe asked after a long silence. He motioned toward the trunk of the car where they'd laid the plastic-wrapped leg. It was beginning to give off an odor.

"They burn everything." Bennie was trying to decide

what to do about the window. If he rolled it up, he could smell that damned leg in the trunk. If he rolled it down, the dump invaded his nostrils. He finally compromised by cracking it a little and filling the air with cigarette smoke as fast as he could. Bennie looked out over the dump where big rats were bouncing out of the refuse, scurrying back into invisible holes. He shivered. Tecate beer or no, at that moment, he wasn't sure he liked being head of the homicide division.

They worked into the night, digging through the rubble, sifting through the contents of a thousand plastic bags, opening soggy shoeboxes, tearing up cardboard cartons. By two A.M., Bennie Montoya was covered to the elbows in coffee grounds and orange peels, but there was no sign of the rest of the dead body. Whoever had been attached to that leg simply was not at the city dump.

It was three o'clock Wednesday morning before he slumped behind his desk at the station and dialed the hospital.

"No, couldn't be," the answer came. "We burn all our amputations."

With that, Bennie Montoya leaned forward and fell asleep on his desk. Slowly, from the distant recesses of his sleep, he heard a tap. He tried to raise himself, but his arms and head were like lead. Around him other sounds filtered through—paper shuffling, a phone ringing, faint laughter. The tapping persisted. Someone's got to fix the washer on that goddamned faucet, he thought. Tap, tap, tap. It was even and measured, coming closer and closer. Suddenly it stopped. Bennie Montoya raised his head. "Jesus," he whispered under his breath.

"Sorry to disturb your . . . uh, nap, Captain Montoya, but I wanted to know if there had been a report on the autopsy."

Bennie Montoya looked at Lexey Jane's eyes. They were bright and glittering from a good night's sleep. She leaned a bit on the cane, her head tilted questioningly.

"Look, lady, I been up all night trying to find the rest of a dead body, and . . . " Immediately, he was sorry. Lexey Jane gasped. "No, no, nothing to do with your friend. I . . . damn! I must have fallen asleep!"

"Would you mind phoning the pathologist?"

"Yeah, yeah," Bennie mumbled. At that moment, a secretary laid a sheet of paper on his desk. "I think this is what you want," she said, glancing at Lexey Jane.

Bennie rubbed his eyes and read down the page. "I know this is going to disappoint you, Mrs. Peltzioni, but your friend died a natural death." He couldn't help it. The old dame brought out the sarcasm in him. "Seems she had arteral . . . arteralss . . . "

"Arteriosclerosis. Hardening of the arteries."

"Yeah. Brought on a cardiac arrest." He smiled.

Lexey Jane sighed and looked around the office for a moment. "Thank you," she said and turned.

Bennie Montoya watched her. The cane tapped rhythmically across the tile floor and as she straightened her shoulders and started down the stairs, he was sorry he'd been so abrupt. She was a pretty elegant old broad.

Lexey Jane paused on the sidewalk to get her bearings. It was a crisp day with clean thin air and a brilliant sun. She took a deep breath. "Don't worry, Peaches. I haven't given up," she whispered. At that moment, a block away, a dog's tail swished around a corner and disappeared. A black and white tail. Attached to a monstrous hairy dog. Snooker!

Lexey Jane started to run, but the pain jerked her back. "Oh!" she cried in frustration. "Damn, damn, damn!" She stood on the walk, hammering her cane against the concrete and cursing the body she was trapped in. Agonizingly, she straightened her shoulders and walked slowly back to the hotel.

When she returned, there was a message waiting for her. She dialed the number and waited for the gruff Spanish accent.

"Mrs. Peltzioni . . . "

"Why don't you just call me Lexey Jane."

She detected a tiny bit of relief in his voice. "Lexey Jane, I'm sorry I barked at you this morning. I had a bad night."

"I understand."

"I was wondering if you could take care of . . . you know, Mrs. Mueller. The funeral," he added quickly, "and if you know the name of her lawyer."

"Yes. It's Julien Strauss in New York. I was just about to call him. I'll have him get in touch with you."

As she hung up, she heard an odd sound from the receiver. It sounded like a belch.

She dialed quickly. "Julien, please contact Mr. Bennie Montoya at the police station here. It's about Peaches."

"Something's wrong. I can hear it in your voice."

"Oh, nothing. I just suffered a fit of pique on Main Street," she forced a laugh. "Do you think you'll have to come out here to settle the estate?"

"I don't know yet. Let me see what I can do from here first."

"Julien, do you have a copy of Peaches' will handy?" She knew it was an absurd question. Julien would have all of Peaches' affairs neatly catalogued, filed and enveloped with those precise little white tabs.

"Yes."

"Read the beneficiaries to me." She heard the crackle of paper on the other end. That's the sound of death, she suddenly thought. Not the dirt clods falling on the casket, or the pealing of bells. It's the crackle of paper. Stocks, bonds, wills, money, old newspaper clippings, faded letters, bent photographs . . . snap, crackle, pop, you're dead. No bang, no whimper, just a crackle.

"Her property holdings go into a foundation to finance a weaving school. At least, that was the last request. Lexey Jane, I know you don't want to believe this, but Mrs. Mueller was the kind to change her will every time she got mad at someone. All right, let's see," he puffed, "TC stock is what we're interested in. Half of that one million was left to a friend, Ivy Boydon. The other half to a nephew who lives in Port Lavaca, Texas."

Lexey Jane crossed her fingers. "His name wouldn't happen to be Jerry, would it?"

"Sorry. It happens to be Andrew. Andrew Mueller."

Lexey Jane leaned back against a pillow. She pulled her lips tight in disappointment. Now, you know that would have been too good to be true.

After she hung up, she called the Boydon number. Summoning all her Spanish, she was able to find out from the maid that Miss Boydon was *en su casa*, but she would not talk, *lo siento*. Señora Boydon was in the middle of a painting.

If I'm standing at the door, she can't refuse to see me, Lexey Jane decided. Ivy Boydon would have to be included in Shiela McCarthy's tour of Santa Fe. As she reached for her coat, the phone rang.

"Lexey Jane," Julien was wearing his conciliatory voice. "What makes you think Mrs. Mueller was murdered?"

"I . . . I . . . just . . . "

"According to the pathologist, she didn't have a mark on her."

"I just know she was, Julien. I felt it the minute I walked in that room and saw her. I felt it!"

Silence. "You've been in Santa Fe too long."

"You have to admit it's a possibility, Julien," she answered angrily. "When I talked to her on the phone, she guessed immediately the stock was a forgery, and then got vengeful and angry. I show up the next day and she's dead. You must admit that's suspicious."

"Not for a sixty-nine year old woman with asthma, emphysema and arteriosclerosis. From the autopsy, it was a miracle that woman was still alive. Lexey Jane, I wish you'd come home. I feel safer about you when you're in Wilmington."

She smiled smugly. Whenever Julien worried about her, it meant she'd half-convinced him.

"Julien?" With one finger, Lexey Jane drew a silhouette of a bearded man in the fine dust on the bedside table. "Can an artist—I mean the kind that paints with oils on canvas—can that artist also be a counterfeiter?"

"It's not likely. It's such a different process, requires an entirely different set of skills," he answered. "Why do you ask?"

"Just wondering."

"Catch that next plane."

"Can't, Julien. I'm on my way to talk to Ivy Boydon."

"Lexey Jane!"

The voice sounded tiny and small as she hung up the receiver.

". . . and Ladies and Gentlemen, you are now entering the famous Canyon Road, the road of artisans." Shiela McCarthy cupped her hand to her mouth as she turned the station wagon up a narrow, winding street. "Supposedly it was an Indian trail to a pueblo, later used by Coronado, Mexican militia, American dragoons, and the Armies of the North and South. Now it is lined with some of the finest galleries in the world, rare antique shops, goldsmiths, silver, turquoise, handmade clothes, and all that tourist crap."

With her cane firmly wedged against the door, Lexey Jane chuckled and allowed herself to relax and enjoy the scene. Shiela inched the station wagon along the serpentine street. Low adobes, closed against the bright sun with faded green shutters, crowded against them as if in some sleepy Moroccan village. At every turn, a ribbon of colored signs hung on standards, from windows, over doors:

The Streets of Taos Gallery
The Silver Bird
Herbs, Etc.
Sunflower Fashions
The Coppery
Glassblower

"To your left is the famous Delgado Street Bridge on which the Rosenbergs were supposed to have passed their atomic secrets."

Lexey Jane glanced down at the short, dusty bridge. What an odd place for intrigue. She tried to imagine Ethel Rosenberg leaning against the cracked concrete railing in the still night . . . it was all so absurd. But it did seem another example of violence that lay beneath the drowsy, dusty streets. Or beneath an enormous poncho?

"One of the nicest problems in Santa Fe is the number of good restaurants," Shiela continued in her Chamber-of-Commerce voice, "and today the tour will dine at one of the world's finest." She turned a sharp left and the car plunged straight down. "The Compound," Shiela announced, pulling up in front of a large white adobe building amid tall pines and cottonwoods. "This was the architect Alexander Girard's *pièce de résistance*," she said with a little flourish of her hand. "A sort of twenty-first-century Indian pueblo." She parked the car near the entrance and came around to help Lexey Jane.

She could not pry her cane loose—the tip had caught beneath the floor covering, and the staff was unrelentingly trapped under the handle. "I can't get this thing . . ."

"What's wrong? Don't you trust my driving?"

"Oh, no! It's just that . . . I must have pushed the silly thing with my foot."

After some coercion from both of them, the cane dropped docilely to the floor between the door and the seat. "Ah, there we are." Lexey Jane smiled uncomfortably.

Inside, a small Lebenese man met them with a weary smile. "Vernon, this is Mrs. Pelazoni from Delaware, Shiela whispered. "First visit to Santa Fe. So we'd like a good table."

He led them by stark white sunlit walls, past two enormous windows framed simply by the painted arch of a rainbow. Rainbows. *Why does a rainbow keep popping up in my mind? The ribbons of colored signs along Canyon Road, the sunlight tossing prisms everywhere I look . . .*

She sat near a cavernous fireplace overlooking a summer patio. Shiela leaned across the table. "I recommend this place to a lot of visitors at the La Fonda. So once in a while Vernon pays me back with a lunch." She laughed softly and took off her poncho.

Lexey Jane was amazed at how tiny Shiela McCarthy was beneath the voluminous layers of clothing. The girl's black eyes darted at Lexey Jane, read the thought. "It's a way of hiding."

"From what?" Lexey Jane lit a cigarette, watching Shiela along the length of it.

"Mmmm, several things. But mostly myself. I had a

nervous breakdown once, started floating on ceilings and disruptive things like that." She spoke mechanically as if to keep some anguish impervious to emotion. "I guess I thought if I wore enough clothes it would hold me closer to the ground." She tossed her hand. "That's how I met Mrs. Mueller. I took weaving lessons from her. The totally consuming craft to keep one from spinning in midair."

Lexey Jane examined her for a long moment. There was an ache far back in her eyes, in the tight, whispery voice that came through with a sad warmth. The girl is harmless, Lexey Jane. "Let me buy you a cocktail, and you tell me who Shiela McCarthy is, beneath all those clothes."

"I'd love a drink, and you can tell me why you think Mrs. Mueller was murdered."

It caught Lexey Jane off guard. The cigarette flew from her twisted fingers and landed on the seat beside her. Shiela ran around the table and pulled at the cushions. A waiter rushed across the room with a glass of water. Lexey Jane painfully tried to leap from a sitting position. With triumphant relief, Shiela at last produced the mangled cigarette. "If we're going to spend all our time extricating you from the perils of everyday living, there's not going to be time for much else." She laughed.

Lexey Jane shook her head, laughing heartily with her. "You surprised me. I forgot I blurted it out to you the day that . . . when I found her."

"Well, I'm not too surprised," Shiela answered.

"At what?"

"That you think she was murdered."

"Why?"

Shiela looked away thoughtfully. "She was your friend. You should know."

"But Peaches was always so dear, such a . . . a . . ."

What had Peaches been? An apple-cheeked flirt at Vassar? A rollicking, roistering companion from the days of youth? Daring, reckless, always a laugh? The daughter of an old family friend? "Tell me how you saw her," she asked.

"She was a Gemini, first of all . . ."

"Do you believe that . . . that astrology stuff?"

"Not really," Shiela sipped her drink. "But if you live in Santa Fe, it's hard not to be bombarded by it. When you meet someone, it's the first question you're asked. And when you tell them—zip—you're categorized, stapled, and filed away." She smiled slowly. "Besides, Mrs. Mueller sort of fit the mold."

"All right," Lexey Jane acquiesced. "What is a Gemini?"

"The Jekyll and Hyde of the zodiac. They lie with great ease because the whole concept of good and evil bores them. And they can be great friends as long as everything goes their way. If it doesn't, watch out. They can cut you to pieces. They're fickle . . ."

"Peaches Mueller?" Lexey Jane gasped.

Shiela nodded. "I only heard Mrs. Mueller blow up once. A young girl came in during one of our lessons. They went into the living room to talk. I don't think I've ever heard anyone hack another human being to pieces like Mrs. Mueller did that girl. All words, but God, what a weapon! If I'd been that girl, I would have killed her. In fact, I remember wondering that day if there was a lawyer good enough to convince a jury that a verbal assault could be as lethal as a gun. Because she killed that girl with words."

Lexey Jane shook her head. She was dazed, her memory too full of another person.

"And when Mrs. Mueller came back into the room with me, she was all sweetness and light." Two black eyebrows arched across the table.

A small moan escaped Lexey Jane. Her emotions rattled inside her like loose marbles. Shiela had shown her another person, one who could cultivate enemies, and she felt sadness at losing an old friend twice. "I'll have to think about this, Shiela. The Mrs. Mueller you're talking about is simply not the Peaches I knew."

Shiela smiled kindly. "I'm sorry. I didn't mean to tear up some memory for you."

"No, no. It's something I must know." Lexey Jane blinked at the plate set in front of her. A thin, golden crepe was folded over the "surprise of the day." Inside that crepe, she thought, is the answer. If I cut into it, I'll know.

Shiela looked sideways at her. "Could I help you in any way?"

"Figure this out?" The moment she answered, Lexey Jane knew she'd bonded herself to this Irish lass. Julien, of course, would be angry. He always chastised her for taking in girls who reminded her of Anne. Posh to Julien! He was far too cautious.

"Frank Parcher would be pleased to work with you."

Lexey Jane had just cut into the crepe. Tiny green tips of fresh asparagus popped out at the end. Oh no! That was not what was supposed to be inside that crepe. Not Frank Parcher. "Frank Parcher?" she exclaimed so loudly a waiter came running with a coffee pot.

"And others," Shiela bowed her head slightly. "But for now, Frank Parcher is enough."

"You can't be."

"I am."

" *Rain Doesn't Kill, The Merry-go-Round, The Mariposa Murders* . . . ?" Lexey Jane shot out the titles of the paperback mysteries and Shiela McCarthy nodded her head at each one.

"It's extraordinary!"

"No. It's money. Money so I can eat."

With a bite of crepe still trembling on the end of her fork, Lexey Jane attempted a bow. Jagged pain shot through her hip. She squeezed her eyes shut. "I would be honored," she whispered.

"Hey, don't go sentimental on me," Shiela said quickly. "I'm Shiela the chauffeur during the day, and moonlight as Frank Parcher. Nothing very grand, I'm afraid."

"I've always wanted to know how . . . ?"

"Well, the hardest part is leaving enough clues." Shiela laughed. "You see, in reality it's fairly easy to kill someone without getting caught. But when you're writing about a murder, you must drop enough clues along the way so the hero can figure it out without looking like an idiot. Of course, there are different kinds of murders. Now, if we're going to form this partnership, tell me something about yourself, Lexey Jane Pelazoni."

Shiela's voice and expression had oscillated so rapidly, Lexey Jane felt dazzled, befuddled, and thoroughly excited. *It's fairly easy to kill someone without getting caught . . . different kinds of murders. . . .* But the crepe tasted so fresh and good, and the warm gin had finally seeped through her bones, that she heard herself laughing easily. "If you're Frank Parcher, then I'm the Nancy Drew of the Geritol set."

"There it is. Up there."

After lunch, Shiela had driven her on into the low mountains of upper Canyon Road. She dipped her head beneath the visor and saw the blue sign hanging out over the asphalt.

IVY BOYDON STUDIO AND GALLERY

"Do you want to go in with me?" Lexey Jane asked.

"No, no. I better wait out here."

Lexey Jane sighed. "All right. I'll be Holmes if you want to be Watson."

"The important thing is that we find Moriarty," Shiela giggled, and snuggled down inside her poncho.

Lexey Jane started up the long, winding steps. They ended at a wooden gate. She opened it. On the opposite side was another row of twisting steps made from stones and railroad ties. At last she was standing high above the road on a tiny porch. She started to knock. "If that door opens out," she thought, glancing over the side, "I'm a goner."

She gave a small smile of relief as the door jerked inward and she looked straight into a baby face that had collapsed with age. The hair was gray and short clipped.

"Yes?"

"Miss Boydon? I'm a friend of Peaches Mueller."

"Come in." The voice was husky and deep.

Lexey Jane stepped into a gallery crammed with easels and tables. Open bottles and tubes of paint lay over the floors, across windowsills, tossed into corners. Huge canvases splashed with wild colors covered the walls. She held her breath a moment against the strong odors of oil and turpentine.

"If you're Peaches' idea of a peace offering. I wish she'd sent a man." The artist laughed huskily and pulled a straight chair toward a table. "Sit," she commanded.

"A peace offering?" Lexey Jane asked, dropping gingerly into the chair.

"Yeah. We had one helluva fight last week. I guess she's told you all about it."

Lexey Jane looked at the woman. She wore faded jeans and her shirt was as paint-splattered as her canvases. She sat down on a small sofa and reached for a pack of cigarettes on the table. Lexey Jane studied the strength in this woman. She had the powerful arms of a sculptor, and for a moment, Lexey Jane imagined Ivy Boydon tossing large blocks of stone as if they were feathers.

"I'm afraid not," she answered. "Peaches is dead."

Ivy flicked a sinewy hand through the air. "Well, I guess it had to happen sometime."

"What do you mean?"

"The asthma and emphysema," Ivy answered. "Doctors told her to stop smoking, but she wouldn't do it."

Lexey Jane shifted uncomfortably on the chair. "Had you and Peaches been friends long?" she asked.

The head tilted back and laughed. "Ever since I married the Count."

"Oh? You're married?"

"Oh, no. That only lasted ten days." She leaned forward and Lexey Jane smelled whiskey.

"You see, after we were married for ten days, the Count decided he wanted to cross the Gobi on a camel. I don't happen to like camels." She laughed again. "I never saw him after that. Divorced him while he was somewhere in the middle of the desert."

Lexey Jane glanced around again. The brilliant slashes of color on the walls pressed against her, taking away her breath. "Do you mind telling me what you and Peaches argued about?"

"Oh, that." She shoved the air with her powerful hand once more. "I needed some money. This hasn't been a good year." She nodded toward the collection of canvases. "And Peaches told me she'd spent all her reserves for some stock."

"Did she say who sold it to her?" Lexey Jane leaned forward eagerly.

Ivy tipped her head. "No. I don't believe she ever mentioned a name. She just said he needed the money for this machine that was going to make her live forever, cure her emphysema and everything else. That was part of the bonus."

"A machine?"

"Well, I got furious. Peaches is . . . was a little . . ." Ivy tapped her temple. "Hardening of the arteries, you know. These last few years I wasn't sure she was always playing with a full deck, if you know what I mean."

Lexey Jane nodded. "Did she say anything else?" She struggled to sound indifferent.

Ivy shook her head. The short gray hair didn't move, as if it were solid, sculpted out of stone. "Oh, something about this machine being the hope for the world . . . a bunch of crap I didn't really listen to because I was so mad at the time. She'd told me she would help me out . . . loan me some of that fortune . . . and then when I asked, it wasn't there! She flicked the end of her cigarette as if attacking the ashtray. "Will say one thing for Peaches. Even if her arteries were turning to rock, she was still a mean, hard-assed businesswoman. She said the stock was worth more than what she'd paid for it. But when I asked her if she could cash some of it in, she blew into a hysterical fit. So I told her to . . . well, shove off. I was tired of her offers that never came through."

"Mmmm," Lexey Jane pondered this for a moment. It was difficult to think in this room. There was something hard in it, coarse and impure.

"I hope you find him."

"Who?"

"The nut she loaned that money to!" she shouted irritably. "That's why you're here, isn't it?"

"Yes, yes," she answered quickly. "I'm afraid Peaches made a rather bad investment."

"Hell, that's what I tried to tell her the night we had the row. I told her I was a better risk."

You may be right there, Lexey Jane throught wryly. If we don't find the counterfeiter, you just may be a better investment than TC stock.

"Did you see Peaches after that?"

Ivy Boydon's head lowered like a cunning bull. She studied Lexey Jane. "No."

"I'm staying at the La Fonda, Miss Boydon." Lexey Jane wrote her name and room number on a slip of paper. "If you remember anything else about the conversation you had with Peaches, please call me."

Ivy took the paper. "Lexey Jane. Funny, I never heard Peaches mention you."

"Perhaps she used my nickname. Duzey."

The gray head lurched back and a full masculine laugh exploded through the room, rattling against the walls. "So you're Duzey!" she choked. "My God! Peaches talked about you constantly!" The head shot forward. "In fact, she talked about you so much I grew to hate you." A thin smirk fixed itself on Ivy's mouth.

"I'm sorry," Lexey Jane murmured. "We had a rather dazzling youth together and I guess Peaches never wanted to forget it." She rose to leave, clutching her purse under her arm.

As she reached the door, she looked about the room once more. What was it in here? What was it that made the hair at the nape of the neck prickle and stand on end? What was it that kept crawling up her spine? She glanced at Ivy Boydon again. The earthen, solid brute strength of the woman glared back at her. It made her feel frail and brittle.

She should have had Shiela come with her. She couldn't make her brain work. She looked at the walls plastered with canvases. Then she knew. The brutal reds, the foaming greens, the boiling yellows flew across the room at her. They were bursting with pure, convulsive violence, bombarding her with their wild, mad frenzy. She shivered and stepped quickly onto the tiny porch. "Thank you for your help, Miss Boydon. I may call on you again."

"Anytime."

The door closed behind her. As she stood, gathering her courage for the long winding descent, something caught her eye in the distance. She jerked her head. A lean man with pale hair was jogging down the road. In tennis shoes and sweatshirt. She opened her mouth to call, but he disappeared around the corner of a wall.

She hurried down the steps, catching the ferrule of her cane in a crack, stumbling, regaining her precarious balance. "Did you . . . Shiela." She tried to catch her breath. "Did you see a young man with blond hair walk past?"

Shiela turned and looked at her. "No. Nobody's been by here except two kids on bicycles."

Suddenly, the door high above them opened and a loud, husky voice called down. "Hey! I forgot. She kept rattling on about a crystal, or crystal. Didn't make sense to me."

"Did she . . ." Lexey Jane held her gloved hand in the air. "Do you know anyone named Iris?"

"No." The door banged shut.

"Iris? What's this about Iris?" Shiela started the car.

"It was one of the names on a list I found at Peaches' home. Does it mean anything to you?" Lexey Jane was still breathing heavily. She put the cane between her knees as Shiela turned the car around.

"Flower. Girl's name."

Lexey Jane sighed. "And crystal?"

"I even knew a girl once named Crystal," Shiela answered, looking at the sky smeared with crimson. In the west, a brilliant blood red glow hung onto the mountains. Shiela fumbled in the folds of her poncho and extracted a large owlish pair of sunglasses.

"Iris, Crystal, Ivy. It's beginning to sound like a nature study," Lexey Jane complained.

She was irritated with herself for allowing Ivy Boydon's paintings to so affect her. "I feel like such a bumbling amateur. What would Frank Parcher do?"

Shiela smiled from behind two black discs. "Frank Parcher would probably say it's time for another drink."

"Ah," Lexey Jane chuckled, "at least in that area, I'm a pro."

Peaches' funeral was set for nine o'clock, Thursday morning. Lexey Jane stalked the hotel lobby waiting for the limousine from the funeral home. Shiela had promised she would drive her to the cemetery, but now this strange, capricious note: "Can't meet you this morning. Please be careful. Frank."

She tugged her fur jacket around her. "Can't count on anyone," she grumbled, pacing the tile floor. Some little whippersnapper of a feminist who passes herself off as Frank Parcher wants to play detective with her, and then disappears! Stop it, Lexey Jane. It's the funeral, and you know it. Too many memories. Black limousines with flags flying on antennaes. First a daughter, then a husband. Friends. And you next, Lexey Jane. Through the glass she saw the car from the Sanchez Funeral Home pull up to the curb. Life is sweet. With all the pain, it is sweet. She steadied herself on her cane. And without the pain how would you know you were alive? The sun is shining.

She sat alone in the back seat of the large car, fearing she might evaporate before they arrived, hanging desperately onto memories of other limousines and other flags when Augustus was at the Court of St. James.

The driver turned off the highway at the dutiful, funeral pace, and into the entrance of Rosario Cemetery. The grass was coarse and strawcolored. Past the bleak pauper's corner with the small tin shields on stakes. Sadly bent, toppled, as if a strong wind had blown them there by accident. Past the old Hispanic family plots with death fenced in squares by iron spikes. Faded plastic wreaths, dead brown chrysanthemums. . .why always chrysanthemums? She must have Julien write that in her will. No chrysanthemums.

The limousine stopped at a Spanish adobe chapel. Over the door hung an oversized rosary, like some cowboy's giant lasso caught on the wall. "Probably lights up at night," she sniffed.

She climbed from the car. The grave was located in a solitary spot with dusty pines and straggly cottonwoods. Lexey Jane looked around. Counting the driver, there were six mourners: the minister, the plump housekeeper who had worked for Peaches, two young men from the Sanchez Funeral Home, and herself. Shiela was right. Peaches had made very few friends. She half-expected to see a spray of irises, but there was only a canopy of white and yellow daisies.

The minister solemnly shook her hand, scuffed and fidgeted for ten minutes waiting to see if anyone else would appear. At last he opened his Bible. Lexey Jane bowed her head and closed her eyes, struggling to keep her mind away

from the coffin, away from the autopsy she'd demanded.
She didn't like to think of Peaches lying inside there in
pieces, like some jigsaw puzzle.

Without warning, she felt the skin crawl along her back.
Someone was watching them. Someone was watching *her*.
She lifted her head slightly and slid her eyes to one side,
then the other. She couldn't see beyond the minister. His
words droned around her: ". . . he who sows to the Spirit
will from the Spirit reap eternal life . . ."

A hoarse scream split the air. Her head bolted upward.
Overhead, perched on a winter-bleached branch, a black
crow gave another rasping *caw*. Then she saw him. Beyond
a fence, a field scattered with crumbling adobes, half-torn
walls, a lithe figure darted across a narrow space. Jerry? She
saw him again, then he disappeared into the pink sand
walls.

Gone! And no way to call out. No way to run after him.
She squeezed her eyes shut. Her frustrated sigh rattled
across the "amens." When she opened her eyes, she saw
the small, strange group staring at her, their faces collapsed
with sympathy.

Chapter Five

Lexey Jane sat on the bed and held one of the hotel drinking glasses. It was an ordinary glass with a slight bulge near the rim, but as she turned it in a shaft of sun, it sliced the light into a rainbow that trembled on the opposite wall. She played with it a moment, scattering the colors across the white plaster.

"I will try it and see what happens," she thought, setting the glass on the table. "I know only one person whose brain is indexed." Sometimes she could blurt out a single word and Julien would promptly click out valuable information.

Crystal. Shiela had suggested a girl's name. But what else? Baccarat? Venetian? A seer's ball? Goblets . . . wine glasses . . . a chandelier . . . the Crystal Palace in London . . . ? She dialed.

"Julien?"

"Lexey Jane, I'm glad you called. I was just getting ready to . . ."

"Julien," she cut him off, "crystal."

She heard the short, puffy laugh. "Odd. Quite odd. There was a strange burglary in yesterday's *Times*. Do you think there might be something to this ESP?"

"Of course there is. Now tell me about the burglary." She could already picture a man in a black mask packing Orrefors water goblets into a canvas bag.

"A crystal skull was stolen."

"A crystal *skull*?"

"Yes. Isn't it odd that you would . . . was it in the papers down there?"

"Julien!"

There was a huff from his end. "Not much information. But if I remember correctly . . ." he began slowly. Lexey Jane could almost see the mental notecards flipping on their spirals. "It was found in 1927 by an explorer named Mitchell-Hedges in Lubaantun, the abandoned ruins of a large Mayan city in British Honduras, while he was searching for the lost Atlantis."

"Are you serious?"

"I knew you'd like the part about Atlantis."

"And so would Holmes. Now go on."

A sigh. "Not much more, really. He kept it until he died in 1959. Then his adopted daughter inherited it. Sometime this week, it was stolen from her home in Ontario. She insists it has strange powers, and that it will bring death to whoever takes it."

"You say it's Mayan?"

"No one's really sure. There are three or four more—one in France, one in London, but they're crude and rough cut, and considered hoaxes. At least Mitchell-Hedges had witnesses when he found his. And supposedly it is most exquisite in its carving. From a single chunk of crystal. I recall that was the great mystery at the time. Archeologists couldn't find a crystal of that size anywhere in the world . . ." She could hear the smile in his voice. ". . . except Calaveras County, California."

"Now I'm supposed to jump like one of Mark Twain's frogs."

"This whole thing may not be full of buckshot, but I'm too much of a gentleman to say what it is full of."

"Your German soberness is showing."

"You ought to be grateful I'm reading the stock market page instead of Edgar Cayce."

"I am, Julien. I am." She hung up.

A crystal skull? Didn't make sense. But then, what did? Frank Parcher was her chauffeur, physics professors were plumbers, stock brokers were streetcorner vendors, artists divorced counts while they were on camelback in the middle of the Gobi desert. Maybe Julien was right. Maybe she should go home. "If I'm not careful, I'll be giving my money away and hand-dipping candles in some commune." But something was holding her in this place, some galvanic force stronger than an obligation to an old friend.

For a moment she let herself sink back into the weight pulling at her. The rattle and clank from the kitchen drifted up through the window. She listened at the sounds, as she'd done in endless days and nights in hospitals. Unconsciously, her ears lapsed into the drowsy game of labeling: a lid wrenched from a can. Slammed down. The precision clicking whirr of a ten-speed in the street outside. A Volkswagen shifting gears. Televised laughter from another room. A cart rolling along the carpeted hall. The spongy tread of tennis shoes outside her door. Hard knuckles drumming on her door.

A small cry of pain escaped her as she bolted upright. "Yes?" she called out.

"It's Jerry."

She grabbed her cane as if to strike this young upstart who darted about, watching her from behind pillars and across cemeteries. "Jerry!" She opened the door and stared into a silver belt buckle. Tilting her head back, she saw two dark eyes looking down at her with quizzical calculation. She hadn't realized he was so tall. He soared above her, blond and gaunt. The man who had been following her wasn't this tall. Was he? But she'd only seen shutter-glimpses of him. There was only one way to be sure.

"Why have you been following me?" She held the door open, but he stood outside in the hall.

"Following you?"

Her eyes whisked over his clothes. Torn bluejean jacket over a sweatshirt, faded jeans, tennis shoes. "Someone dressed like you has been watching me."

"Couldn't be me." He shook his head, then glanced down at the jeans bleached in light blue streaks along his thighs. "If it was someone dressed like me, you got a lot to choose from around this place." Suddenly, his chin tilted, and his eyes swung to one side with a flash of thought. "Interesting," he murmured.

"Well, I thought it was you. Come in. Don't stand out in the hall."

A shiver ran the full length of him, then his face burst into a smile. "Thought you might like to see our pyramid and tell us more about Edgar Cayce. Uh . . . and . . . uh, Annie wanted to make it up to you. Getting all heated up the other night . . ." He flung his long arms out to the side in a shy, helpless gesture and laughed winsomely, as if to apologize for all the angry young women in the world.

Lexey Jane caught herself smiling back at his lanky warmth.

She settled into the front seat of the old pickup, heard

the door screech shut, and saw Jerry tie the rope around the handle outside. Suddenly, she had the uncomfortable thought that maybe this was one of those stupid things Julien was always warning her about. And Shiela.

How did she know this handsome young man was not capable of doing her bodily harm, as they say in courts of law, after it's too late? Jerry tossed her a winning smile as he shifted gears with the sun sparkling on the blond hairs across the back of his hand. And what about that other thing they're always warning you about these days? Rape. Now that, Mrs. Holmes, is a startling thought.

She glanced back at the trail of blue smoke billowing from the exhaust. "Where's Snooker?"

"Home with Annie." His foot pressed down hard on the accelerator, leaving a ribbon of smoke floating down the highway. He turned onto a narrow, blacktopped road, clattered through a village, then shuddered and clanked in a stiff right turn down a dirt road that zigzagged on the brink of some eroding chasms. She tried to gauge the miles. Twelve? Fifteen?

"You're rich, aren't you?"

Lexey Jane felt the cold air rush through the rope-tied door at her side. Was that why she shivered? Or was it the twist of Jerry's mouth as he asked that question?

"Rich enough, I guess. Why?" In front of them, the mountains rose serene, veiled in snow.

"Oh." His shoulders humped in a lazy shrug. "Anyone who could get Edgar Cayce to work on one of their oil wells has got to have lots of money."

"That was my father."

"You didn't meet him?"

"I was a young girl at the time. He seemed like just another confused old man to me."

Jerry's eyes squinted at her in disappointment. "I could tell by your luggage."

"What?"

"That you're rich."

She recalled with what disregard he had tossed her suitcases into the pickup that night. Well, one-for-one, she thought vengefully. "I've got a question for you, Jerry Kirwen." She paused. He didn't look at her. It was the right name—the one in Peaches' address book. "Did you know a woman named Peaches Mueller?"

His head ducked slightly, but he kept his gaze on the road. "Sort of," he answered. "I gave her some plants once. Some herbs I'd raised in the pyramid."

Plants. Poison. Ah-hah! Stop it, Lexey Jane. Your brain is beginning to sound as rattled as this old clunker pickup. The autopsy showed no evidence of poison in Peaches. Besides, how would this boy have the wherewithal to obtain an expertly forged stock certificate? And why would he want a million dollars? Now that's silly. Everybody wants a million dollars. Still, he's—she glanced at him, one elbow lopped languidly on the open window, the other hand gracefully wheeling the rattletrap over bumps and dips— he's not the type. Well, Lexey Jane, it looks like murder is out for Jerry. Sighing, she smoothed her skirt over her frail knees.

"Did you know she was dead?"

"Yep. Read it in the paper." The old truck careened onto another dirt road, slamming Lexey Jane against the uncertain door. "Well, there it is!" he announced jubilantly.

She caught her breath. The truck slid to a stop. Sure enough. There it was. A plywood simulation of the seventh wonder of the world. The raw unpainted wood soared to a point among tall pines. Near the top, windows had been cut into the sides. They caught the sunlight obliquely, like mirrors.

Jerry helped her from the truck, and she stood for a moment looking up at it. Suddenly, she was at Giza, a few miles west of Cairo. In the distance was the western fringe of the vast Libyan desert. And she was gazing up at stones fit together with such precision one could not slip a hair between them. Something was wrong. Something was wrong with time out here. It tricked her at every revolution, turning her counterclockwise.

"Cheops would have been pleased," she mumbled, and hobbled toward the door, passing an old tire hanging from a rope in a tree. She shook her head. The swing seemed oddly misplaced.

Jerry opened the door and she stepped through.

"Hello," someone called out to her in a voice that pinged against the high windows.

Lexey Jane blinked. Rising from a cloud of colored pillows in the center of the floor, a goddess shimmered toward her. Her blonde hair floated in an aura. The light from the windows converged on this creature, exploding with radiance.

"Annie?"

A tinkle of laughter caracoled through the air. "It's me."

"You look so . . . so different." Why won't things stay the way they are, she thought exasperatingly. Why do they keep changing? Nothing—nothing out here is as it seems to be. What had happened to that savage creature who had banged her fists against the world that night of their first encounter? Here, in her place, was this dazzling transformation.

"It's the pyramid," Annie tossed her head. "A day inside it does wonders. I'm afraid you saw me at my worst the oth-

er night. I'm sorry." She folded her slim legs and sat Bud-
dhalike on a fat pillow. Books lay around her in a circle like
rays.

"Inside the pyramid?" Cautiously, Lexey Jane felt her
way into an object resembling a partially collapsed balloon.
The air played around her as she sank into it, air vibrant
with the pungent scents of basil and mint and oregano.
Above, the slanted ceilings dripped with plants in hanging
pots, and in a far corner, she spotted Snooker, asleep, a big
fur rug.

"I'm trapped, she thought. I've lowered my old brittle
body into a vinyl clam shell which would tear all of O.J.
Simpson's ligaments if he tried to bolt from it. In the corner
is a dog who could snap me up like one gulp of Alpo. And
I'm fifteen miles from civilization in some half-baked isos-
celes triangle. What happened to her solid, logical chaise
lounge in Wilmington, the wicker breakfast tray, the stack
of charities? They were real, weren't they?

"The secret is inside the pyramid," Jerry called to her
from a counter that jutted out from a sloping wall. The sur-
face was clustered with smaller cardboard pyramids of all
sizes. He lifted one and pulled out a bottle of wine.

"I didn't believe it either," Annie was saying as she
shuffled a pile of books at her feet. "Jerry's always got some
crazy idea he's working on, but this—" She looked around
her. "I like living here."

"And it makes cheap wine taste expensive. Here."

Lexey Jane took the glass from Jerry, breathed in the
bouquet, then sipped it. "Not bad," she agreed. "How does
it work?"

"Somehow a sort of electromagnetic field is created if a
pyramid is placed on a north-south axis. Any size pyramid.
Doesn't matter. A Frenchman named Bovis found some

dead cats in the Cheops pyramid, and they had *mummified*."
Jerry's eyes glittered. "Then a Czech radio man named
Karel Drbal started messing around with pyramids. By accident one night, he set a small cardboard one on top of some
rusty razor blades. The next morning they were sharp
again—like new!"

His voice roused Snooker. The immense dog lumbered
toward Lexey Jane and thrust a wet nose at her ankles. I
don't understand, she thought. I don't understand any of
it. Godzilla is licking at my toes while that young man drifting around in the sunlight is talking about sharpening razor
blades inside a pyramid. "I don't understand," she murmured.

"Neither does anyone else," Jerry went on. "But there
are a lot of people working on it. 'Course, if you build one
here in this area, you've got an advantage because we're
right in the middle of a ley."

"A what?" Nothing was sounding right. Was he speaking
English?

"A ley." He spread out his long arms. "A path . . . a
kind of magnetic current that follows a line around the
earth. You know, an alignment like the ancient paths mi-
grating birds use. People used to build sacred buildings on a
ley. No one in his right mind would have plopped a building down just anywhere without first using geomancy—a
kind of magic for finding just the right spot on a magnetic
path where all the currents of energy were right. The Chinese still use it. Called *fung-shui*."

Music was coming from somewhere. A blurred, distant
Gregorian chant whispered through her brain. "Where is
the music coming from?" She couldn't move her head. The
drowsy weight of it pulled her backward. Her eyes slid
around the walls. That sound. Where was it coming from?

She'd heard it before—during a bad long distance connection—that uncertain, elusive, haunting melody humming over the wires.

If they would turn up the volume, I could name it right off. Handel . . . no, a bit of Brahms now . . .

"It's the sound inside a pyramid," a voice answered from the center of the room.

A pyramid-sound, she mused, listening. Not Bell Telephone at all. What was that remarkable passage in the Bible about the force of sound being used to tumble the walls of Jericho?

It was the wine, of course. The altitude, naturally. In a moment I will be just fine.

"Your arthritis is better, isn't it?"

With tremendously slow, drowsy effort, Lexey Jane pulled her head forward. She had told no one about the arthritis, about the pain. The pain. Where was it? She had to find that wracking, jagged pain again to come back to reality.

They sat together, the two of them. Watching her. No, they were floating in the sunlight on a cloudbank of rainbows with transparent eyes, and mouths smiling like enchanting myths.

I'm the game and they're stalking me.

The thought darted through her mind so rapidly it left her with only the shudder.

"I've said nothing about arthritis." There. That was a crisp retort. That'll fool them, make them think I'm alert and on my guard.

"Well, I . . . your cane, the way you walk. I just guessed it." Jerry seemed flustered. Beside him, Annie nervously flipped the pages of a book.

"About those razor blades, Jerry. Why were they sharpened the next morning? What happened?" Her voice droned inside her ears, in and out with the melody.

"It's pretty complicated, and I'm not sure anyone knows for certain. But the razor blade is a crystal structure . . ."

Listen! Lexey Jane commanded herself. Close out that damnable music. Feel the old pain. Come back, Lexey Jane! He just said the magic word. Listen.

". . . if it's put in this electromagnetic field, the crystals are . . . well, rejuvenated, I guess you'd say. It's what happens to a human being inside a pyramid. We're full of crystal structures, you know. And they get rearranged in the right way."

I will keep him talking. Maybe he's right, perhaps the secret is in this plywood thing somewhere. "Inside the king's chamber in the Cheops pyramid," she struggled with the sentence. Her voice was sounding strange again. ". . . I remember the walls and ceiling were covered with slabs of rose-pink granite. Granite is a crystal, isn't it?"

"Very similar to germanium," he answered, sitting forward on his haunches. "Scientists do know they can slice off a piece of germanium, then trigger it with an electromagnet, set it into motion—vibrating, you see—and that tiny little slice will generate some mysterious energy for infinity."

"Germanium?" Why isn't it *Iris*?

He shrugged. "It's an element, like silicone."

"This energy coming from that little piece of crystal—what does it do?"

"Everything," he answered quickly. "It can cure cancer, emphysema, hardening of the arteries, and . . ." He grinned impishly at her. "Arthritis."

Suddenly, Annie slapped the book shut. Lexey Jane flinched at the sharp pistol shot of pages hitting together. A bolt of pain rushed through her hip. She smiled at it. A good sign.

"This is boring. Can't we talk about something else?" The young goddess glanced around the room.

"No, no," Lexey Jane protested, "I'm fascinated."

"Annie's right. I find someone who'll listen to me and I start running off at the mouth. Only one more thing and I'll shut up." He looked guardedly at Annie as if she might explode again. "There's a scientist in Bordeaux, France, who's working on one of these crystal machines, and . . . and there's a physicist somewhere around here working on the same thing."

"I'd like to meet him." Ah, there. Her voice was real again. Gravelly and hoarse.

Jerry chewed his lip. "If I can find where he's hiding, maybe . . ."

"Hiding?"

"The government's after him."

"Why?"

"The rumor is that he can turn metals into gold with the energy from the crystal."

Be nice, Lexey Jane. "Alchemy, mmm." She hid her cynicism behind a sip of wine.

"Every one of us is a bundle of atoms and molecules speeding around and around, okay?" His pale eyes widened. "But we're held together in a human form by some secret. So, to get gold, you just have to learn how to rearrange the molecules. I think the Egyptians knew how to do it. There was a capstone on the pyramid, you know, and it was made of crystal. I believe that had something to do with it."

A crystal capstone. The words hummed around the room. A crystal skull, perhaps? A crystal skull with its facets of cheekbones, jawline, the axes of the forehead all trembling with secret energy and turning the streets to gold. Poor Cortez, she mused. He was looking for the wrong thing all the time.

"Jerry, did you ever speak to Mrs. Mueller about this?"

Her question split the air. Annie's head whipped around. She glared at Jerry. The long, lanky body shuffled to its feet. "Dunno . . . talk about it to anybody who'll listen."

A hand was coming for her. It pulled her to her feet.

"Annie's got a test tomorrow. Gotta study. Guess I better get you back."

"Oh? You're in school? I thought . . ."

"When I'm not working at the Legal Tender. Just a literature course. Trying to finish up a degree I started a long time ago."

Lexey Jane studied the girl who smiled shyly at her. She was beautiful. Her blonde hair shimmered in a wave behind her as she rose from the pillows. For one fleeting second, Annie appeared suspended in the air in that graceful motion. "Don't forget your cane," and she held it out to her.

"Thank you." Lexey Jane glanced down at the book nearest her on the floor. She poked it with the tip of her cane. "Now that's a healthy little piece of deception. Poor Othello. Duped at every turn."

"Have to read it. For class." Annie's mouth twisted into a teenaged grimace. She was real again.

Outside, the air was silver with dusk. Lexey Jane watched the tall youth amble ahead of her to wrench open the door of the truck. I'm envious. The thought startled her. I'm jealous of the suppleness of that body, the effortless way it moves, bounding ahead of me. Is that why runners come here? Looking for some secret before it's all over with? Is that what captured Peaches? A rearrangement of hope instead of the molecules?

Jerry helped her in, wrapped the rope around the handle, and gave it a final tug, wrinkling his nose with pleasure over this simple accomplishment.

No, silly. Peaches bought that stock because of a lifelong vengeance. But what if someone promised her more than vengeance in return? What if they offered her youth?

Ahead of them, the sky deepened with rust. A lavender haze sifted across the vast horizon. The old truck rattled into the outskirts of Santa Fe where the sunset was doing its own alchemy on the flat-topped adobes. The huddled houses radiated like pink gold as they sped past. She had just turned to ask Jerry if he could put her in touch with the physicist who could make gold out of lead, when the truck careened around a corner. The door flung open with a grinding wrench. Fingers dug into her thigh. Things were sliding past her hands . . . torn seats and gear shifts and dashboards and windshields . . . flesh was banging at her like hammers. The sound of machinery ground to a halt. Her head cracked against something hard, splintering the light.

"You okay, señora?"

The soft Spanish whisper floated in front of her. A young Chicano boy held her in his arms. She could smell the pavement.

"My God! Are you all right?" Jerry was leaning down, scooping her up like Jell-O.

She couldn't speak. A scream was still hanging on the roof of her mouth.

"She hit her head," the Chicano said.

Lexey Jane looked at the two black eyes scanning her scalp. It was the bellboy from the hotel. There were other people gathering around now. She groped about, struggling against Jerry's iron hold. "Put me down!" she commanded.

Suddenly, a huge black bird swooped out of the crowd. "Damnit!" it screamed shrilly. "Get that mess of junk fixed!" Shiela was slamming at the door hanging onto the truck. "You could have killed her!"

"I . . . I thought maybe that's what you were trying to do." Lexey Jane managed a grim smile at the boy.

"You're kidding I . . . I don't want to lose you." He grabbed her elbow and opened the door into the lobby. "Come on. I'm going to walk up to your room with you."

"And then we're going to call a doctor," Shiela shouted behind them.

"No doctors! I'll be fine in a minute."

"I've got to pick up someone for the hotel. Stay in your room until I get back. Please! If Mrs. Mueller was really murdered, and you're running around town trying to find out who did it, then you're not safe!" Shiela growled in her ear. "Don't you understand that? It's a small town!"

With Jerry at her elbow, she limped along the hall. They reached her room and Lexey Jane gripped the knob. Just then, the door flew open and, still holding the doorknob, she tumbled inside.

"Lexey Jane! I thought we were going to stop this sort of thing," Mannie laughed, catching her in his arms.

"Per . . . perfectly all right," she gasped through her pain and surprise, "I just went flying in the opposite direction a few moments ago."

Mannie turned a hard curious gaze at the boy in the doorway.

"Oh, Mannie. This is Jerry Kirwen. Somehow introductions keep getting caught on the wind in this place." She sank onto the bed. "We just had a small accident."

"The door of my truck fell open and Lexey Jane . . . ah

. . . fell out." Jerry ducked his head in that embarrassed, apologetic gesture of his.

"Are you all right?" Mannie rushed toward her and threw a threatening glower at Jerry.

"Fortunately. Yes. What . . . what are you doing here?"

With that abrupt exchange of emotions, Mannie clasped his hands together in childish joy. "Looking for you. Just finished my first painting, and I wanted you to see it."

She squeezed her eyes shut as a new pain shot across her shoulders. "Tomorrow, Mannie. Right now I think I'd better lie down and convince my bones that the worst is over."

"Sure. Sure, I understand." The forehead lowered into the brutal scars. "You'll be okay?" He looked menacingly at Jerry.

"I'll be fine."

Hesitantly, he opened the door. "You know, you really ought to lock this thing," he said over his shoulder.

The moment Mannie was gone, Jerry jumped to efficiency. He stacked the pillows against the headboard and commanded her to lie back against them. "For someone who just dropped into town, you sure know a lot of people."

"Mannie? He was on the same train. We sort of bumped into one another."

"There," he plumped a pillow behind her head. "Can I get you anything? Water? Aspirin?"

"You can get me that physicist you were telling me about—the one who can cure everything with his crystal machine."

"I'll see if I can find him," he answered seriously, then plunged a hand inside his jacket. "I got a magazine for you." He extracted a small pamphlet and dropped it beside her. "There's an article about him."

The lamplight fell across the cover. *Beyond.*

Jerry was half out the door when Lexey Jane's eyes dropped to the address label in the right-hand corner. "Annie Mueller, Tesuque, New Mexico."

"Jerry! What is Annie's name?"

He frowned. "Andrew. But, damn! Don't tell her I told you. She hates it."

"Then Mrs. Mueller was her aunt. Why didn't you tell me?"

He leaned slack against the door, then ducked his head sheepishly. "Annie didn't get along too well with her aunt. That's why I didn't say anything. Uh . . ."

"Why? Why didn't they get along?

"Annie and I aren't married. That upset her aunt. So she'd take Annie out of her will, then put her back in if she happened to have a good day. Kept Annie pretty stirred up. She needed some money for school and all. So Annie stopped seeing her. Hadn't seen her in months." His head came up with a defiant glare.

Lexey Jane studied the unlined face, the wide-set blue eyes, the pale hair that fell over his ears. So innocent. But was he? How much did he know? Know about what, Lexey Jane? You don't know a hell of a lot yourself! "What about Annie's father?"

"He's dead. So's her mother."

"I know. I know. But her parents were wealthy . . ."

He had already begun shaking his head. "They disowned her. Some family fight. Mrs. Mueller asked her to come live with her and they got into a row right off the bat. Weird family. A bunch of hotheads."

"How can I get hold of you?" she asked.

"We don't have a phone, but I'll keep in touch."

She felt the bruises begin to throb with a new pain. Was it an accident that the rope broke? The grinding tires shivered through her. "Why did you take me out to the pyramid, Jerry?"

His eyes opened wide. "I thought you'd like to see it. I mean, someone whose father knew Edgar Cayce . . . you know what I mean." He winked as he closed the door behind him.

She listened to the squish of his tennis shoes fade down the hall. No, Jerry, I'm really not sure what you mean, she thought, rubbing the growing welt on her head. For a moment, she thought it was her blood knocking against her skull, but it was someone at the door.

"Come in."

"Señora?" The full brown face and black eyes peered around the corner at her. "You have a message."

"Ah, thank you. And thank you for saving my life a while ago."

"*De nada, de nada.*" He backed out the door, smiling. "You okay?"

"Yes."

"You must lock your door, señora."

She looked at the front of the envelope. No stamp. Hand delivered. She tore it open.

"Just heard the tragic news of our friend, Mrs. Mueller. Know you want to discuss legal matters with me. Could we meet at 8:30 this evening in the bar?"

It was signed Rudy Hiatt. Rudy Hiatt. The "R.H." on Peaches' list! A gasp of pleasure escaped her. I've found Jerry Kirwen, Ivy Boydon, Andrew Mueller, and now R.H. That leaves only Iris. We're finally getting somewhere, she chortled. She quickly dialed Rudy Hiatt's number. "Mr. Hiatt? This is Lexey Jane Pelazoni. I guess Peaches must have told you about me."

"Yes, yes." He was panting.

"I'm sorry. I hope I didn't disturb you. I got your note and . . ."

"No, no." The voice gulped air. "Didn't disturb at all . . ."

"I am most anxious to meet with you this evening. I'll be there at eight-thirty."

"Fantastic," came the youthful reply.

"Is there . . . is there anything you might want to tell me before we meet? I'm going to call Mrs. Mueller's trustee in New York, and . . ."

"No, no. I think this is something we must discuss by ourselves."

Lexey Jane hung up, chewing her lip thoughtfully. She propped the pillow behind her before calling Julien. Suddenly, her hand stopped on the soft foam rubber. She squeezed it with her fingers. It bounced "Othello!" she gasped. "If I wanted to murder someone—someone with emphysema, someone whose arteries were clogged and who was teetering on the brink of a heart attack, I'd smother him. Like Desdemona."

She sat up and imagined the beautiful Annie floating above the colored pillows, hovering in the center of the pyramid with the sun shimmering off her. She recalled the night they'd given her a ride into Santa Fe. The exasperation in the girl, the furious, uncontrollable anger at the stalled pickup. Was that enough violence for murder? Yes, she sighed regretfully. I suppose so. But it's everywhere I turn. Ivy Boydon's paintings are full of it. Annie Mueller just might be . . . even chauffeurs who are parttime writers just might be . . . But Ivy Boydon and Annie both had reasons. They thought they had a claim to the money. And that's what counts, Mrs. Holmes. Motives. As Julien would say, it's who *benefits*.

She reached over and dialed. "Julien? What made you think Andrew Mueller was a male?"

"What would you think if someone wrote you a letter and said, 'I want to leave a half-million to Andrew Mueller, my brother's only child'?" Julien's voice snapped. Either something unpleasant had happened or he was miffed at having his competence questioned. "Now what assumption would you make?"

"Well, Andrew Mueller is a girl," Lexey Jane cooed soothingly, "and happens to be living right here in Santa Fe. Well, not exactly in Santa Fe. In a pyramid outside of town." She could see his thick eyebrows folding together.

"Now tell me what you know about pyramids."

"Before or after Napoleon?"

"What?"

"Let's see. The Cheops pyramid at Giza covers thirteen acres, which is the equivalent of about eight blocks in downtown London or Chicago. When Napoleon was in Egypt, he estimated there was enough stone in this single pyramid to build a wall around France. Which might have been his smartest move. That wall would have been ten feet high and one foot thick. It was also one of his soldiers who found that famous yard-long slab, the Rosetta Stone. And it was his army of intellectuals who compiled the *Description de l'Egypt,* nine volumes and twelve books of drawings and engravings."

Lexey Jane chuckled at the stream of information. She sometimes wondered if Julien had encyclopedic print running through his veins instead of blood. "How do you know all this?"

"You own stock in IBM, don't you?"

"Yes, but . . . ?"

"The IBM 1120 is being used at the pyramids. I'll go back

a little. The Nobel Prize physicist Dr. Luis Alverez developed a method of measuring cosmic rays in the pyramids at Giza. The smaller pyramid of Chephrem was selected for the experiments, sponsored—by the way—by the U.S. Atomic Energy Commission and the Smithsonian Institution. They moved in the IBM to computerize their recordings on magnetic tape. In looking after your interests, I checked into it."

A tingle rode down her spine. "And? What did they find?"

"So far it's been a failure."

Lexey Jane slumped back against the bed. "A failure?"

"The project has turned the entire University of Cairo into a bunch of pyramidiots. Each day the computer comes up with a different recorded pattern."

"Oh, Julien, say it so I can understand it."

"Let's see. It's like sending two plus two through the machine every day, and every day you get a different answer. In other words, the computer has been unable to computerize the data they've collected. Does that make sense?"

"As much as anything else I've come across the last three days. Oh, Julien, I wish you had time to go to Egypt."

"Damnit!" The expletive exploded in her ear. Totally unlike Julien. He never swore at her.

"What is it?"

"Well, you got me off on crystals this morning, and now pyramids! We are trying to trace a forged stock certificate, as I recall."

"Don't be snide, Julien."

"By the way, I was looking at those stocks again last night, and recalled another case in which the forgery was so excellent it fooled everyone. In fact the only way it was ever discovered was by a clerk performing some arithmetic on the number of bottles."

"Bottles?"

"Wine," he answered. "In 1973 three men allegedly bought up the harvests of Languedoc-Roussillon, not far from the Bordeaux region. But the grapes from there are inferior to the Bordeaux grapes. So they forged the documents certifying the grapes' origin. Then they labeled them Bordeaux *appellation controlée.*" He chuckled. "Caused quite a scandal. Used to be that if you even *stole* a bunch of grapes in Frances, you lost an ear."

"Go on. What about the bottles?"

"Well, they labeled some two and a half million bottles." And when the clerk began adding up the harvests from the Bordeaux region, his arithmetic didn't figure. There just wasn't any way for that much wine to come out of the Bordeaux vineyards. That's when the investigation began. Odd thing was, by all reports, the wine was fairly decent."

"Do you think whoever forged those wine documents also forged the TC stock?"

"I'd like to agree with you that anything's possible. But it's highly unlikely."

"Julien, get me a bottle of that wine. And a bottle of real Bordeaux." She softened her voice. "You can do that, can't you? Send them out here?"

"And just what do you have in mind?"

"A plan, Julien. A tiny little plan. Might not work, but . . ." Bordeaux! That was it! "Julien!" she cried excitedly, "there's a scientist in Bordeaux who is building a crystal machine that will cure cancer, arteriosclerosis, make you young again . . ."

"Do me a favor," Julien cut in dryly, "I have to be in court the next three days. If you won't come home, will you please stay in your room?"

She contemplated the austere voice in the receiver.

Well, she certainly couldn't tell him about meeting Rudy Hiatt at eight-thirty, now could she? She glanced across the bed at the small magazine Jerry had given her. *Beyond.* Beyond. "Julien, it all might fit together. If Peaches had a Ponce de Leon soul, if she was searching for some fountain of youth, then she could have loaned the money for another reason."

"Won't work, Lexey Jane. Mrs. Mueller was a businesswoman. She learned that from her late brother. And hope is not a tangible collateral."

"There's something about this place that makes you think it is."

"It is a *non sequitur,*" he clipped with uncommon exasperation.

"Don't sound so definite, Julien. Oh, guess who took me to lunch? Frank Parcher."

"Who?"

"Frank Parcher, the author of those mysteries I like."

"Those mysteries you read belong in the three percent I refuse to remember."

"Only he's Shiela McCarthy in real life. A woman! Can you imagine that?"

"Then have a bookstore deliver some of those mysteries, and stay locked in your room for three days."

"Take an aspirin and call you in the morning. I know."

"Lexey Jane, you are not Sherlock Holmes. You are real and this blasted situation is real. I don't know if there's any real danger to you, but my God, why take risks?"

"All right, Julien," she murmured meekly and hung up. Within minutes it rang sharply at her side. "Hello."

"McCarthy, you said?" Julien sounded anxious.

"Yes."

"Tim McCarthy was married to a Shiela McCarthy, a minor writer. I thought the name rang a bell. There was a big smear in the papers about it."

"About what?"

"One of those Colorado millionaires. Land speculation. Shot himself about a year and a half ago, and left everyone in the lurch. Owed a couple of million. But . . ." he hesitated, "there was some question about his wife. For a while she was suspected of murdering him. But it was judged to be suicide, so she was never brought to trial."

Lexey Jane held the receiver away. Her mouth would not close.

"Lexey Jane?"

"Yes, Julien," she replied weakly.

"Stay in your room," he warned. "Don't go to any more lunches with strangers. Do not get into any cars . . ."

She squeezed her eyes shut, felt the lump on her head, then forced her voice to a light tease. "Oh, Julien, they don't take you 'for a ride' out here," she assuaged, "they take you for a long walk on a short mesa."

She hung up and tried to take a deep breath. Shiela? Tiny Shiela with her pounds of clothes holding her down to earth? It was like asking her to suspect her own daughter!

"Oh!" She grabbed the magazine at her side and pounded it on the bed. "Ridiculous!" She flipped the pages until she found the article. Two small paragraphs were devoted to a Dr. Filiamo in the Santa Fe-Los Alamos area, how he'd tried to patent his machine, had performed experiments for federal agents who supplied the lead and kept the gold produced by the radiant energy of the germanium crystal. How it could cure cancer, how the government demanded the secret without offering payment. Bitter and disillusioned, Dr. Filiamo had gone into seclusion. And a footnote about the cancer machine in Bordeaux.

So this is where Jerry got his information. From a pulp magazine. She leafed through the pages. I want to believe it. I wish I could believe it, but the advertisements! A vibroscopic divining rod for $6.95 and a four-inch crystal ball for only $49.95, "Unconditionally guaranteed." A telephone number to call if you sought "prosperity," albums of meditation music which "takes you beyond this universe," a course in super-hypnotism, a brain-wave synchronizer, Twelve Good Reasons to Buy This Horoscope. But the most tempting was an ad for a surefire formula to predict the outcome of horse races!

She plopped the magazine on her lap. How hungry the world is for hope, she thought. So starved they will buy it from a magazine for $49.95, unconditionally guaranteed. And maybe I'm no better. She shook her head. Poking around in corners where I don't belong , sniffing out suspicious people with a victorious glint in my eye when all the time they may be perfectly innocent. Nuts maybe, but still innocent. Julien is probably right. And that Captain Montoya as well. Peaches probably died in her sleep.

She reached for a cigarette, lit it, and smoked slowly. And Peaches probably didn't spend a million dollars on a forged certificate at all. It's my stock that's the counterfeit. And I hoodwinked Julien into thinking it was Peaches' so I could make some sentimental journey on a train.

The cigarette tasted bitter. She stamped it out. But, no matter how you looked at it—66666 or 99999—one of those certificates is definitely a forgery. No "beyond" about that.

She closed her eyes. *Non sequitur,* Julien had said. Doesn't follow. It ain't necessarily so.

Far back in her drowsiness, she heard the sound. Tap. Tap. Tap. Water dripping.

She pulled her eyes open and looked at the portable

clock. Oh, no! It was eight-thirty! She would miss Rudy
Hiatt if she didn't hurry. She threw her legs over the bed.
"Ah!" The pain was back. Razor sharp. Fumbling for her
cane, she lifted herself slowly and hobbled into the bathroom.

Something cold and wet hit her feet and a streak of light
crackled up her cane. Glass is breaking. Glass is breaking
all around me into tiny splinters, sharp and full of fire. It's
breaking inside my bones. And I'm rising to the ceiling, just
like those pilots who go shooting from cockpits. But my
blood is boiling and my skin is too tight. Why can't I keep
my mouth closed? It keeps jerking back against my teeth.

The iron taste of blood filled her throat.

Someone was screaming. The high, shrill whine keened
through her ears.

A strong, putrid odor of burning flesh caught in her nostrils as a weight crushed against her chest, pounding her,
pummeling her down through the floor.

Chapter Six

His office on the top floor of the police station was a long way from the john. But it had a view. From Bennie Montoya's desk, he could see the clouds moving in over the mountains, the storm coming down from the Rockies. With one eye still watching the swift gray mass, he answered the ringing telephone. "Montoya."

"This is Dr. Logan at St. Vincent's. And, well, I think I owe you an apology. You know that leg you found?"

"Yeah."

"Well, I amputated it. And the fella wanted to keep it. Said he was going to carve something out of the bone."

"Jesus!"

"Well, it was *his* leg!"

"We dug up the whole city dump, Doctor."

"I know. I'm sorry. I called him and he said the thing got to smelling so bad, he decided to throw it away. How did I know it was going to land on top of the dump?"

"You didn't. Only next time let me know, okay? I've got some papers here you'll have to sign. I'll run 'em over before the storm hits."

Bennie looked at the brown grocery sack on his desk. He picked it up, set it down. Oh hell, as long as he was out he'd just run it by the hotel, leave it at the desk for that Lexey Jane. That way he wouldn't have to face her again.

The hospital was first. He parked outside. On the second floor, he found Dr. Logan, who avoided his eyes and abruptly signed the papers Bennie laid in front of him. He was waiting for the elevator when the short, plump nurse approached him. "Bennie?" She was the daughter of an old friend. He'd known her since she was born. "Marie! Good to see you." There was the faint smudge of a smile beneath his mustache.

"You haven't been around here much lately. But I guess that's good." She laughed. "Bennie, we got a patient last night, and she keeps asking for you. Do you have a minute?"

"Who is it?"

"A Mrs. Pelazoni." Marie saw Bennie's eyes widen. "Do you know her?"

"Sort of. What happened? Heart attack?"

"No. She was electrocuted."

She was waltzing.

It was 1934 in Berlin, at the Aden Hotel. A young Nazi officer had asked her to dance. "Certainly," she'd answered brightly. And they had waltzed and waltzed, and waltzed until Lexey Jane felt the perspiration flying from her. But the music went on. "Can you reverse?" he asked. "Certainly," she'd answered, delighted because her head was dizzy. At last he begged to sit down. And the tall Baroness with the short upper lip had turned to Lexey Jane "He paid the orchestra to keep playing until you gave up." And Lexey Jane had laughed. "I never give up."

She heard a slight sound in the room and opened one eye. "Mr. Montoya," she whispered.

"I was over here at the hospital . . . if I told you why you wouldn't believe it."

Wouldn't I? I would believe anything now.

". . . and the nurse said you were here . . . been asking for me."

"Someone tried to murder me."

The big man shoved his hands deep in his pockets. His mustache quivered with exasperation. "Lexey Jane, it just isn't so. That hotel has old wiring and there was a leak somewhere."

"Someone knew about my cane . . . that it has a metal tip . . ." It was difficult to talk. Her whole body felt limp.

"It was an accident! Pure and simple." He shook his head. "You got to stop going around thinking everybody's been murdered." He drew his hands from his pockets and threw them into the air. "Why would someone want to murder you?"

Lexey Jane bit her lip. "Can't tell," she murmured.

He ignored her. "Well, I'm glad you're all right. Listen, I got some of Mrs. Mueller's things in a sack in the car. Was going to bring it over to the hotel to you. But I'll send it up." He quickly ducked out the door.

Lexey Jane could hear him outside talking to the nurse. "I wish those dames would stop watching so much television. Jesus! From the voltage she got, she must have a heart that won't stop."

"I do." Lexey Jane smiled to herself. "I do."

The odor of old damp fur wafted in and out of the medicinal smells. She opened one eye. A bear was standing in the doorway. Or was it Snooker? No. It was Frank Parcher in her raccoon coat with a scarf tied around her head and a floppy hat perched on top of that.

"You're awake?" Shiela McCarthy tiptoed toward the bed.

Lexey Jane took a breath. She choked on it. The bruised pain in her chest was too intense.

"Hurt? I'm sorry. I electrocuted a character in a book once, and in my research I discovered if you pounded on the heart, you might get it going again. I guess maybe I overdid it."

"You saved my life?"

In one motion, Shiela emerged from the oversized coat and waved her small hand in annoyed embarrassment. "Well, I wouldn't go so far as to say that. Thank God, you fell backward onto the carpet. Sort of unplugged yourself, I guess." She grinned. "I'm just glad I didn't break a rib."

She looked funny. Small and tiny boned, she stood at the end of the bed with the enormous hat shading her like a worn-out umbrella. Lexey Jane tried a smile. "Shiela? Tim McCarthy. Does the name mean anything?" She'd scarcely got out the words before Shiela gripped the end of the bed with both hands.

"Not yet," she choked. "Can't talk about it."

Instantly she whirled and grabbed the coat, engulfing herself in its safety once more. When she turned back to Lexey Jane her face was brittle with cheerfulness. "I have to go. You'll be all right here."

She was halfway out the door. "Shiela!" The soreness heaved through her chest. "Do you think someone tried to kill me?"

The tiny face peeked around the corner, furrowed in a frown. "I don't think it was an accident."

"Do something for me. Find out who was in the room above me."

"I already have. There is no room above you."

"Come back!" But she was gone. The nurse appeared in the door.

"Did you call, Mrs. Pelazoni?"

"No, no." She clenched her fists and mumbled to herself. Why was it all so topsyturvy? It started with those damned certificate numbers being upside down. And since then nothing has been right side up. Now you have every reason to assign a jim-dandy-doodle motive to Shiela-Frank-Parcher-McCarthy. A husband commits suicide, insurance policies won't pay off, couple of million dollars in debt. She's intelligent. And she has the wherewithal to get forged stocks; that is, *if* she didn't murder him.

But she saved your life, Lexey Jane. Pummeled your heart back to a waltz. What was it you said to Julien? "Counterfeiters don't murder people." She started to roll on her side. Her sore body forced a cry to the roof of her mouth. "Do they?"

Rudolph Hiatt was a type of endangered species indigenous to the Santa Fe area. An unidentified visiting sociologist had once classified the genus as "formers." Having reached the top of their professions, they had—because of age or too much smog or too much traffic on the freeway or whatever—sought the recuperative values of the desert in self-exile. There was the former princess who owned the Hope Diamond for six days before her check bounced, the former mistress of Eugene V. Debs, a former tap dancer with George White's scandals, a former shadow to Ted Lewis . . .

. . . and Rudolph Hiatt. He stood now in front of the full-length mirror. He did it quite often, even though he was an old man—old enough to have been the former head of guerilla operations for the OSS during World War II. But he was still lean, trim, no sign of a paunch. And he still had his hair, thinning, but enough to grow it below his ears and keep it a pale blond with color rinses. Even had his eyes fixed to remove the pouches. And he could still brag about hanging a wet pea coat on an erection—an image that definitely dated him for the younger crowd who might have believed this braggadocio had Rudy Hiatt said "shepherd's coat" or even "mackinaw."

Rudy Hiatt detested giving up his youth.

Dressed in his favorite outfit of faded jeans, sweatshirt, and sneakers, he turned to the side. The derriere was still firm. Smiling with satisfaction, he left his house and jogged up Canyon Road. By the time he returned, the newspaper was in his box. What he read on the second page threw him into a violent rage.

"Goddamn! Goddamn!" He wadded the newspaper and threw it against a wall. If Rudy Hiatt had maintained his youthful appearance artificially, his explosive temper had needed no plastic surgery. It was the one he was born with. And it was deadly. After whirling around the room, kicking the coffee table, pounding his fist against his palm, he slumped into a chair, spent with his own fury.

It was a scene identical to one earlier that week.

With Peaches Mueller, he'd acted rashly, stupidly.

"I believed in you!" she had screamed over the phone. "It's counterfeit! You're nothing but a cheap crook!" And then a coughing spasm had seized her.

He had grabbed his pistol and driven out there. No hard-assed female was going to send him to prison. He would kill her. His cloak-and-dagger soul conceived of every possible way to murder the old bitch. He would wring her neck, he would shoot her, he would beat her over the head, torture her, leave her body woven in and out of that goddamned loom of hers . . .

But when he arrived, she was already dead. Poised, hands folded neatly in her lap, she stared at him with lifeless eyes. The irony of it had made him laugh. It shook his whole body. His head flew back and he'd laughed until it rang through the empty house. He was safe. He was safe! Hell, he'd been safe all along! As fortunate as Peaches Mueller's death was, it was unnecessary. It didn't matter what accusations she shouted. That counterfeit was so expert no one could tell it from the real thing. "Fool!" he'd cried.

"Goddamned fool!" he shouted at this moment, kicking at a chair in his living room.

Then the Pelazoni woman had come. If Peaches Mueller knew the certificate was a forgery, then so did someone else. Someone had to tell her. But who? The old woman who hobbled around on a cane? At first, calmly and methodically, he had spied on her, watching her trips around Santa Fe. But at night, he would fly back and forth in his living room like a broken pendulum.

There is no possible way for her to know.

But someone knew. Someone told Peaches Mueller.

Was it the old lady?

Fool! There's no way anyone could know!

But she must have been suspicious. Why else would she be here?

If she is suspicious, then she knows something.

Then—

He saw her with Mannie Ringer in the La Fonda bar.

Following an eruption during which Rudy Hiatt destroyed his footstool and a fireplace screen, he sat down with a double straight scotch. From his early training he knew it was foolhardy to kill someone who might be of value later. And Mannie Ringer was an asset. Besides, the Frenchman had said "hands off." Deduction and conclusion? Killing the old woman would be less suspicious. (And easier to perform, although his ego would not let him admit this.)

Planning it brought on a nervous excitement he hadn't felt in years. A public place. Yes, above all, public. The La Fonda bar. Always crowded around eight. He'd be there early enough to get a table. And wait. Wait with the curare. So easy to tip into a half-finished drink in the darkness of the bar. The curare itself had pleased him enormously. A toxin used by South American Indians to tip poison darts, it had been easy to obtain from a veterinarian because it was used as a muscle relaxant for animals.

He relished the sentimentality of it. The OSS had used derivitives of curare during his espionage activities. Just stop breathing. They just stop breathing. And no way to detect it in the body. A trillionth of a gram. Los Alamos had a machine that could spot it, but who would think to drag an old crippled dead body up there to that lab? It was just like old times.

He waited in the La Fonda bar through two drinks. Until he saw the commotion in the lobby. Then in total stupefaction, he watched as they carried Lexey Jane out on a stretcher.

"Heart attack," someone said in the flurry.

In his living room now, he glanced again at the small item in the paper. "Tourist Survives Accident in Local Hotel." And further down, ". . . revived by an unidentified visitor."

"Ahhhh!" Rudy shouted at his stereo. The toe of his

sneaker hit a plant and sent the clay pot flying. Dirt sprayed over the carpet. For the second time in a week he had been thwarted. For one who had survived the very worst of a world war, it created within him a strange juxtaposition of emotions. As if the failure of his plans was somehow equated with growing old.

Now he would have to tell the Doctor. At least talk to him, try to explain. Warn him. The gift he had would help.

He slipped on a windbreaker, gingerly picked up the package from the floor of his closet, nestled it firmly in the front seat of his car, and backed out of the garage. The storm clouds still swept the sky, blocking out the moon. He drove north toward Tesuque, then cut to a roller-coaster dirt road that took him through dry riverbeds, bouncing over deep ruts. He put a hand on the package. Then the road twisted off to the right at a fork. He stopped as the headlights beamed on a high fence. Pulling the emergency brake, he got out to open a crude gate.

He had just forced a wire loop from around the fence post when he heard a sound. He cocked his head and looked back at the car, listening to see if the running motor had made the strange growl. Turning, he dragged the gate open just as something leaped at him from out of the dark. He had no time to cry out. The weight crushed against his chest. He had only time to clutch his arms around the flesh he'd so protected and pampered before it was torn from him.

"I will not ride in an ambulance!"

"But Mrs. Pelazoni, you're not strong enough to . . ." the nurse coaxed.

Lexey Jane glared at the bone-white van in the emergency entrance. Her eyes twinkled. "It's against my religion."

Shaking his head, the attendant slammed the rear door shut. "That's one I never heard before."

"It's only a few blocks to the hotel. I'll walk."

"I can't let you go by yourself."

"Then you go with me."

"I'm sorry, Mrs. Pelazoni, I can't leave. I'm on duty."

"Then call the La Fonda. Ask for Shiela McCarthy."

The nurse sighed. "All right. But you have to promise me you will wait right here."

Lexey Jane could hear her whispering to the attendant as she walked away. "What kind of religion is against ambulances?"

Lexey Jane smiled. Thank the Lord I'm in Santa Fe where anything goes. I could never have got away with that in Wilmington. The truth was she had never liked ambulances. Long before one had taken away her husband Augustus, she had disliked them. Even before that, they had smelled of death.

But when Shiela drove up in an old sedan, Lexey Jane regretted her eccentricities. "It's one of those days," she said breathlessly. "Wagon broke, so they gave me this clunker . . ." Lexey Jane became snappish. The days in the hospital had left her considerably weakened.

"I could have walked."

"Now, don't be silly. Get in the car and prepare yourself for three blocks of sheer adventure," Shiela cooed in her whispery voice. "Grab hold of something. The clutch is shot."

Lexey Jane gripped the handle as the car lurched and bounced toward the hotel like a broken spring. She was beginning to review her aversion to ambulances when Shiela pulled up in front of the entrance. "I'm going up with you," Shiela said as she helped her from the car.

"Good. I think it's time we talked. Don't you?"

"Depends on the subject."

Shiela opened the door to the room, and before either of them proceeded further, they both cautiously checked the bathroom. The wiring had been neatly repaired and painted over. The tile floor was dry as a blotter. "Mmmm. Well, at least your misfortune has left the world a better place in which to live." Shiela smiled. "Hey, someone's sent you a present. And flowers!"

A spray of mums fanned out on the bureau in profuse apology from the management. And next to it lay a neatly wrapped package.

"From Julien," Lexey Jane read the return address. "Punctual as usual."

"Julien?"

"My lawyer and broker." Lexey Jane considered the attractive, petite woman for a second. Do you think Julien would like . . . ? No. She was always trying to match him up with someone who was altogether wrong.

Shiela's dark eyes narrowed. "Are you going on with this stupid search, or did the shock treatment work?"

"Not on my curiosity," Lexey Jane answered with quick defiance, "but it fried a perfectly good cane! Crisp as a breadstick."

Shiela put her hands out defensively as if Lexey Jane were going to poke her with a mental image. "This whole thing about Mrs. Mueller . . . does it have to do with money? A great deal of money?"

"Even for Frank Parcher, that's pretty astute."

"I . . . I overheard her talking to that girl, the one I told you about. Mrs. Mueller said something about it being 'only a loan.'"

"Do you remember anything else? Did she say what it was for?"

"I'm sorry." Shiela ran a hand across her forehead and

up through her hair. Suddenly, she was far away, preoc-
cupied. "I can't remember anything more. Just that I was
horrified by the fight they were having."

"Shiela? Why did you come to my room the other night?
Thank God, you did, but why?"

"Someone was at the desk asking for you."

"Mr. Hiatt," Lexey Jane murmured dismally. She'd
phoned and phoned him from the hospital, but no answer.
She'd lost him again.

" . . . said he was to meet you. I thought I'd wander up
here and walk down with you. The minute I opened the
door, you fell out of the bathroom, the phone started ringing . . . it was madness!"

"The entire affair is madness," she mumbled to herself.
"Who was on the phone?"

Shiela's eyes widened in astonishment. "I didn't answer
it. Sorry, but I was trying to get your heart to beat."

"Oh dear." Lexey Jane rumpled her hair with her hand.
"I'm afraid I've suffered brain damage."

"I hope so. Maybe that will put us on the same level."

Lexey Jane grinned weakly. "And you say there's no
room above mine?"

Shiela leaped from the chair and ran to the bathroom.
"They've plugged it. Look here. There was a hole drilled in
the ceiling, but it's been fixed and the watermarks painted
over. After I got you to the hospital, I came back here and
looked. There is no room above yours."

"I want to see for myself."

"You sure you feel like it?"

No, Lexey Jane concluded, she definitely would not introduce Shiela to Julien. What if it worked? What if they
liked each other? Then she'd have both of them after her.

In a moment, they were on the third floor standing before a blank white wall. "See?" Shiela held out her hand.

"Wait a minute." Lexey Jane tottered back to the corner and began to tap the wall with her knuckles. The dull thud of adobe changed abruptly to a hollow echo. "There *is* a room behind there," Lexey Jane almost shouted. She looked at Shiela. The girl's face was expressionless.

"Let's go back to your room. I'm going to check something," she said slowly.

"Now stay right there," Shiela warned her, as Lexey Jane sat on the edge of her bed. "Don't move. Don't even go in the bathroom. I'll be right back. And for God's sake, start locking this door!"

Lexey Jane rose and opened it gently just in time to see Shiela disappear around the corner. At the far end of the hall the "exit" sign glowered at her with a dull, defeating, reddish haze. She locked the door, unlocked it, measured the interminable distance between imaginary flames, and mumbled, "I'd never make it. I'd end up a chitling." She closed the door and sat back on the bed.

After five minutes, Lexey Jane began to tap her feet. After ten minutes, she started tapping her fingers on the bedside table. She lit a cigarette, finished it. Lit another. At last she saw the doorknob turning.

Shiela's face poked through. "I told you to lock this!"

"You told me not to move!" Lexey Jane shouted back at her.

Shiela began to laugh. "Do you suppose Holmes and Watson had these problems?" She closed the door behind her and unrolled a yellowed sheaf of papers.

"If they did, I understand why Holmes took up cocaine. What have you got?" Lexey Jane reached for the papers.

"I've got a little marijuana, if you'd like to try that?"

"Shiela!"

"Only kidding. Look what I found. Took a little digging. But I remembered seeing these one day in the office. The old plans for the hotel." She sat on the bed next to Lexey Jane and they held the crackling paper between them. "Look here. On the third and fourth floors, rooms have been sealed off."

"Why?"

Shiela gave a Spanish shrug, "Who knows, señora?"

"But it doesn't make sense."

"Somewhere in the recesses of the mysterious Spanish mind and the enigmatic Indian soul, there was once a reason."

"How old are these plans?"

"Dunno. But I do know the new manager wasn't even aware that he had six more rooms to rent."

"Is there any way to get to them?"

Lexey Jane watched Shiela's finger trace the sepia-colored lines across the paper. They were such small hands. How could they be capable of murder?

"There's something here. A door of some sort." Her nail jabbed at a diagonal line. "Want to go back and see?"

Lexey Jane grabbed for her cane. Her hand clutched air. "I miss that cane." She bit her lip. To think her balance in the world depended on something the size of a dime.

"How about an arm?" Shiela offered.

On the third floor, they walked straight toward the narrow door hidden in an irregular corner. Shiela took hold of the knob. "Are you ready?"

Lexey Jane looked askance at her. "If either Dracula or Charles Laughton jumps out of there, I hope I can remember how to scream."

Shiela shook her head. "I regret to inform you they are

both dead. If anything jumps out of there, it will be the Creature from the Black Lagoon."

She yanked open the door.

They both groaned in unison.

"Not even a mummy," Lexey Jane sighed wistfully.

They both peered into a shallow closet not much wider than the few mice-chewed brooms it held. At the rear was a long board that had been loosely and rather sloppily nailed. "It would take someone pretty small to squeeze through . . ." Shiela felt the sharp eyes on her. She turned and stared straight into Lexey Jane's curious gaze. "Hey, wait a minute. I don't like that look. Not at all."

"No . . . I didn't mean . . . how well do you know Mannie Ringer?"

"Why do you keep asking about him? What's your interest in that man?"

"You seemed on rather intimate terms with him."

"Because I told him how to make his jeans fit?" Shiela laughed harshly. "I'm afraid we've got a generation gap on that word 'intimate.' He was cheerful and friendly when I picked him up at the Lamy junction. Wouldn't let me touch his suitcase, insisted on carrying it himself. A real gentleman. And I haven't seen many of those lately."

"He was in my room the night I was electrocuted."

"You're kidding," she breathed.

"I surprised him. He was leaving just as I opened the door."

"I told you to keep that damned door locked."

"Funny. That's what he said too." Lexey Jane pursed her mouth. "Could he have got through that space?"

Sheila looked at her wickedly. "Even if I did tell him to get in the shower with his jeans, I didn't exactly measure him."

She closed the door, took Lexey Jane's arm, and they slowly walked back down the stairs. As they reached the second floor, Shiela's head suddenly fell back in laughter. "This is crazy! I've been murdering people on paper for ten years, and this is the first time I've ever actually looked for one."

"The murderer, you mean?"

"No, I don't mean that at all. Aren't we really looking for the *murder?* We aren't even sure we've got one of those yet." She opened the door to Lexey Jane's room and slumped into the chair beneath the windows.

Lexey Jane sat on the bed, both of them in silence. "Do you own any Transcontinental Communications stock?" she asked suddenly.

"Used to." Shiela rubbed her face hard. "But it's gone. Everything's gone."

"Did you by chance sell it to Peaches Mueller?"

The tiny face twitched as if it were sending data through a computer. "So that's it. Mrs. Mueller bought some TC stock that isn't . . . isn't somehow right. Forged, maybe? Counterfeit?"

"Splendid. Is that the Frank Parcher mind at work?"

Shiela sat straighter, absorbed in the game. "And you came here to see if Mrs. Mueller could give you any information about it. But she was dead before you could talk to her. How am I doing?"

"Superb."

"And you think Mrs. Mueller was murdered so she *couldn't* talk to you. And let's see . . . Ivy Boyden . . . good friend of Mrs. Mueller . . . said something about crystals or crystal. Let's see, I wasn't completely with it that day, but Mrs. Mueller loaned the cash on the TC stock for something to do with crystals." She halted a second, her hand in midair. It fell suddenly to her knee. "Now you've got me. Crystals. Radio? Television? They use crystals to transmit waves . . ." Her voice dwindled off and she shook her head.

Lexey Jane looked at her watch. "In about five seconds you have come to the same conclusion which has taken me nearly a week."

"Well, I wasn't electrocuted in the interim. That did use up a few days. What time is it?"

"Nearly four o'clock."

Lexey Jane looked up from her watch to see Shiela rising. The poncho foated like black wings before the window. It was moving toward her, a tiny, batlike face fixed on her with a strange, sad smile. It swooped down at her ankles. She could feel the strength in the small hands as they wrapped around her legs. They were lifting her off the floor. A spasm of regretful fear raced through her. *I've been murdering people for ten years . . .*

"There. Get your feet up and lie back and rest." Shiela was saying, drawing the spread up over her. She caught Lexey Jane's eyes. "I'm sorry. I didn't mean to frighten you. It's habit. I used to do it to . . . to Tim when he was tired."

"Just startled me," Lexey Jane mumbled, angry with herself. Julien was right. She always worried about the wrong things.

"You can trust me," Shiela whispered. She leaned down and pecked her on the forehead. "I'll be gone until tomorrow afternoon. You stay right here. Use room service."

"What is all this? Why do you keep disappearing?"

Her face locked into a blank stare that fixed on a far corner of the room. "I'm trying to protect the last thing I have."

She heard Shiela lock the door as she closed it. "And it's probably the opposite of anything I could imagine," Lexey Jane thought to herself. She waited a few moments, then unlocked it and carried the package to the bed. She unwrapped it, folding back the thick layers of padding around two bottles. In Julien's unerring, meticulous fashion he had tagged each one. Lexey Jane removed them and set the real Bordeaux directly behind the counterfeit Bordeaux on the bureau. "For future reference," she said, tapping them with her finger.

Next, she dumped the contents of the paper bag and spread them over the bed. She'd gone carefully through Peaches' things in the hospital. But she kept hoping she would find something else. Credit cards, comb, driver's license, some loose change and bills. Two copies of *Beyond*—the one with the short article on Dr. Filiamo, and another extolling the paths of glory to mystic experiences. And loose sheets of notepaper—drawings and sketches of future rugs or tapestries, with Peaches' artistic measurements neatly penciled alongside precise lines. She looked again at the one that particularly intrigued her. In the upper right-hand corner was a large polyhedron and below it, a pyramid. The lines crossed the page zigzag fashion, with stars scattered here and there. Colors to be used were written at the bottom. White, yellow, blue, green, orange.

Lexey Jane lay back, exhausted and disappointed.

It was still early evening when she heard the knock. Feebly, she climbed from the bed and answered it.

A human trumpet fanfare greeted her. "Ta–daaaa!"

Mannie Ringer stood in the doorway holding a canvas wrapped in tissue paper. "If Mohammed won't come to the mountain, then the mountain will come to Mohammed." He executed an exaggerated bow, thrusting the canvas in front of him. "Where have you been? I thought maybe you'd left without saying goodbye."

"I've been in the hospital." Lexey Jane smiled at his exuberance.

"What? The old arthritis?"

"No." She watched his face carefully. "I think someone tried to kill me."

Lexey Jane saw the bearded face screw into sincere shock.

"You're kidding!"

She told him of the faulty wiring, the leak from the ceiling that had flooded the tile floor, how the metal tip on her cane had acted as a conductor. But as she talked, his face relaxed as if he truly believed her suspicions were unfounded. He's either innocent or a damned fine actor, she concluded.

"What's all that?" He pointed to the debris spread over the bed.

"That's some of Peaches Mueller's things the police delivered to me." But Mannie looked only mildly interested in her encounter with death and her grocery sack inheritance. His attention was on the wrapped canvas still in his hand.

"Well? Are you ready for this?" He began to tear away the tissue.

"Wait!" Lexey Jane raised her gnarled fingers. "Before the unveiling, there is always a toast." She nodded toward the bottles on the bureau. "There are some glasses in the bathroom."

"Great idea," Mannie exclaimed. He came back with the two glasses and set them on the bureau.

Did she imagine it? It was all so fast. And she had prepared herself! Did he glance at the labels? Did he see something she couldn't see? Mannie Ringer had definitely passed over the first bottle, reaching behind with difficulty for the real Bordeaux. She was certain he'd only glanced at them.

Mannie poured the wine and handed Lexey Jane a glass. "To the first original Emmanuel Ringer!" he declared and downed the entire contents. Then he grabbed the canvas and ripped away the tissue with a flourish.

Lexey Jane gasped.

A young girl in a flowing, pale yellow robe was running— no, leaping— through a field. Her legs danced wide and her arms stretched into the air with tumultuous joy. She was suspended between leaps, caught forever in some innocent exaltation. And the detail! She reached out for it, to touch the soft folds of material, to feel the grass.

"It's a *trompe l'oeil*." Her fingers recoiled from the damp canvas. Only paint and linen.

"A what?"

"*Trompe l'oeil*—deceive the eye. A technique of painting." Her mouth fell open. She turned to Mannie quizzically.

"Is that bad?" he asked.

"No, no. It's quite good. It's just that . . . I suddenly remembered something. How much is it?" she asked quickly. The painting glowed at her. The colors refracted off the canvas in a thousand rainbows, telling her something, all whispering at once.

"You mean you want to buy it?"

"Of course," she answered briskly, "how much?"

"Well, I . . ." He shrugged with pleasure. "Five hundred?"

"Sold." She couldn't take her eyes off it. "Mannie, I'm impressed. You're good. Very good."

He looked at her confidently. "*I* always thought I was."

The painting had done something magic to them both. Lexey Jane felt herself buoyed along the top of her pain, lifted with the reckless, defiant joy flying across the canvas. They laughed and talked nonsense until the bottle was empty. Mannie reached over and opened the other one. The counterfeit.

Lexey Jane tasted it. Not bad. "Mmm. I think this is better than the other bottle."

Mannie shrugged. "All the same to me. I just drink it."

But she had gone too far. She knew it the minute he turned to her. The beard trembled. The face tightened. The scars on his forehead jumped forward.

"Better be going," he announced. "Let you get some rest."

"I want to walk down with you Mannie. The doctor said I must walk as much as possible to get back my strength," she added hurriedly. She couldn't let him leave like this. She would lose him forever. And it was too soon. Too soon. "Your check. For the painting."

"Oh, yeah."

Oh, her stupidity! Watching him with crouched, suspicious eyes while she called attention to the wine. She must learn to do these things with more finesse. She had drained the excitement from him, put him on his guard. Or had she? She'd seen Mannie Ringer's peculiar moods before.

She chattered aimlessly as they walked down the corridor, joked about the elevator; they made faces in the mirrors lining the wall, so that the tension had eased a bit when they reached the lobby. She walked with him to the outside door.

"Ohhhh." Lexey Jane clasped her hands. A light snow was falling. It piled in thick, silent layers over the low adobe roofs. The full moon laid a silver light over the streets and buildings, and the large, soft flakes floated down through it. She sighed with pleasure. "Robert Frost and Walter De la Mare would have loved this night," she said, then chuckled, "if not each other."

"Why do you do that?" Mannie asked.

"What?"

"Always think of someone in the past. Like the other day on the park bench. Talking to yourself about all your old friends."

"I don't know. My love of the past, I guess. Or maybe it's because the past is so *real*." She laughed gently. "Whenever I fly, just at takeoff, I think how Leonardo da Vinci would have loved riding in that plane. He wanted to fly so badly. And when the astronauts were landing on the moon, I hoped Jules Verne was somewhere watching." She saw the snow cling to Mannie's beard as he stepped out the door. "I feel like they're all friends I owe something to—a thought, at least. A memory," she sighed wistfully.

"Julien?"

A series of unintelligible mumblings came through the receiver. "What time is it?"

"Only nine-thirty here. Oh dear, I woke you. It must be eleven-thirty in New York."

"And I have to meet my client at six in the morning."

"This will only take a second. I need your brain. Harnett."

"*Trompe l'oeil,*" he answered yawning.

"Ah," she sighed with gratitude. "Harnett's first name. What was it?"

"William, I believe. Just a minute."

She heard bumping and shuffling. In a moment, Julien was back turning pages of a book. The receiver scraped against his shoulder. "Yes. It was William Harnett. Died in New York City, 1892. Worked as an engraver in Philadelphia . . . probably from this activity that he learned the infinite precision that raised his art above that of the *trompe l'oeil* naturalism at the time. His painting of a $5 bill was considered close to forgery."

"Didn't you say an engraver couldn't paint successfully with oils?"

"I said it was unlikely."

"But possible."

Julien gave a conciliatory sigh. "As you say, anything is possible."

"Thank you, Julien. Call me when you're through in court."

"Wait a minute! Now that I'm wide awake, would you please explain this nocturnal interest in art?"

Lexey Jane looked at the painting sitting on the bureau. Even in the dim lamplight it was really quite good. Extraordinarily good. But something still disturbed her. "I can't explain it, Julien. Not yet. To borrow a phrase from my father, at the moment everything is half-assed backward."

"*That* I understand."

Lexey Jane hung up and examined the painting again. "I have the feeling we've met before," she spoke to the girl leaping across the canvas. "Wishful thinking," she grumbled.

She scooped up Peaches' purse and papers on the bed. "Forgive me for putting you back in a paper bag, Peaches, but it's the best I can do at the moment." She picked up the empty sack and looked into it. A grocery receipt was stuck to the bottom. "Lexey Jane, you fool! Holmes would never forgive you." She pulled out the sticky paper.

Her heart sank. On the back were the initials R.H. and

Rudy Hiatt's phone number. "Posh!" she shouted, then bit her lip. "Maybe it's a reminder from Peaches." She dialed the number she had been trying for two days. Still no answer.

She looked at the clock. Nine forty-five. She dialed Ivy Boydon. The lusty voice boomed out of the receiver. "Hello."

"Miss Boydon, it's Lexey Jane Pelazoni. Uh-
. . . Duzey, Peaches Mueller's friend. I'm trying to locate a Mr. Rudy Hiatt. Do you know him?"

The voice exploded sarcastically in her ear. "Rudy? Sure, I know him. He's got cirrhosis of the ego, that one! Another of Peaches' nutty friends."

"Do you know if he acted as her attorney here in Santa Fe?"

"Hah! He'd like to think so! But I kept telling Peaches the bastard never saw a law book in his life!"

Lexey Jane blanched. "Do you know where I can contact him?"

"He's in the book. Call him."

Lexey Jane hung up and smiled sadly. She had the odd sensation that for Ivy Boydon everything in life was either black or white. And that was a strange feeling to have about an artist.

At 7:30 A.M. the following morning, Saturday, March 6, Lexey Jane dialed the number again. She made little solicitous noises with her tongue, and listened to the interminable ringing. Still no answer. She tried every ten minutes. At eight o'clock, she dialed another number.

"Mr. Montoya? Could you help me locate a person by the name of Rudy Hiatt?"

"Won't be hard," Bennie replied. "He's over at Sanchez Funeral Home."

"He's dead?" Lexey Jane crumpled.

"Like in doornail."

"I demand to see the body!"

Bennie Montoya glared over his mustache. "You have no right to see the body!"

"I have reasons to believe this man was involved in Mrs. Mueller's death."

"Look here, Mrs. Peltzioni! Everybody who dies in Santa Fe is *not* murdered!" He found himself shaking his fist at her. He'd never done that to an old lady!

"It's Lexey Jane! And everyone in Santa Fe does *not* die of a heart attack!"

Bennie Montoya leaned forward on his desk, and put his hand over his mustache. "I can't let you see the body," he mumbled from behind his hand.

"Why?"

"Because they're trying to patch him up."

"Patch? What do you mean?"

He'd thrown her with that. He was in control again. He took his hand away from his face. "Because he was pretty torn up. Some animals got hold of the body."

"Lexey Jane gulped. "I would still like to see it . . . him," she insisted.

"I can have you thrown out of here, you know."

For the first time since he'd encountered her, he saw Lexey Jane lean toward him with an impish grin, her eyes twinkling mischievously, and say, "But you wouldn't, would you," with such charm that even Bennie Montoya had to admit the whole act was appealing. He shook his head helplessly. "I'll call and see if it's okay"—his eyes flicked up at her—"to review the remains."

Rudolph Hiatt was dressed in a dark blue suit and laid out

on a work table in the back room of Sanchez Funeral Parlor. A sheet had been drawn over him to keep the adobe dust from settling on the expert repair job. Bennie Montoya gingerly drew it back from the face. Small, bluish sunken spots of decomposition had been powdered and rouged.

Lexey Jane sucked her breath.

"You know him?"

"No. I've seen him before. In the La Fonda. The night I arrived." Had she? It was so dim in the bar that first night with Mannie. And her attention had been on the other face—the spatulate one she'd seen in a book somewhere. She peered down. Was this the specter who kept disappearing behind pillars and adobe walls?

"How old is . . . was he?"

"Round seventy something. One of those health nuts. Jogging all the time. We found him up in the hills. Probably gave out, and then . . ."

"Did *you* know him?"

"Sort of. He used to come into the station all the time. A real crackpot. Wanted to do undercover work for us. Said he'd worked in the OSS during the war."

"Does he have any family?"

"None. I've traced everything. Wife dead. No children."

Lexey Jane studied the powdered face. Near the right ear several deep pits had been filled in. There was a similar indentation on the chin. She swallowed loudly. There was no collar to the shirt Mr. Hiatt was wearing. Instead there was a white binding made to simulate a turtleneck sweater. She had the uneasy feeling that not much was left beneath it. If I could only open those eyelids, she thought. But you don't go around opening dead people's eyes, remember? You close them. Still, if I could, I have a strong feeling they would be filled with surprise and horror. "What's that around his neck?"

Bennie rolled his ink-stained tongue. "That is to hold his head on, Mrs. Peltzioni," he answered with measured defiance. "The throat was torn out."

"I want to see all of him."

"What?"

Before he could stop her, she grabbed the corner of the sheet and flipped it back until Rudy Hiatt lay in full view. She looked at the trim athletic figure, then at the pale hair. "He could have been the one." She nodded.

"What do you mean?"

"The man who was following me. Spying on me."

Bennie rolled his eyes to the ceiling. "Jesus!" he whispered.

Lexey Jane tapped her finger on the table next to Rudy Hiatt's sleeve. "Mr. Montoya, do you think it's possible . . ." Her eyes strayed to the arm. She blanched. The cuff was empty. The hand was missing. Completely gone. Torn off at the wrist. She jerked her fingers away. ". . . that he could have been killed *first* by some animal and then left to die?"

"Of course. I get you," he answered cheerfully. "You're trying to tell me this guy's been murdered. Right?"

"Precisely."

"Look, lady!" He flung out his arm. "We got a whole library down the street chuck full of mysteries. Why don't you go get some of those, curl up in your room, and get your kicks that way. Instead of bugging me!"

For the second time, Lexey Jane looked up at him with twinkling eyes. "Because this is more fun. The real thing is always better, don't you agree?"

* * *

Shiela was at the desk when she returned to the hotel. "Shiela. I must talk to you. Immediately."

"The bar's not open yet. Let's sit over here in the corner."

"I've been to see Mr. Hiatt, Peaches' attorney," Lexey Jane whispered excitedly.

"And? What did he say?" She looked fragmented, tired, blue half-circles beneath her eyes.

"Nothing, I'm afraid. He was dead."

Shiela whipped around, her face twisted in disbelief. "You're kidding."

"I wish everyone would stop accusing me of that."

"How? How did he . . . ?" Sheila put up a hand. "No, don't tell me."

"Well, of course, the pathologist says he died of exposure, heart attack . . . and then animals got hold of the body."

Shiela could not suppress a smile. "I can see you don't believe any of it."

"No. No, I don't. I think something caught Mr. Hiatt by surprise, and it was not a heart attack. I think it's possible that he was killed first and then left to the elements."

"But what makes you think that? What are you going on?"

"A hunch." Lexey Jane chewed her lip.

"Not enough."

Lexey Jane leaned into her face and whispered. "His throat was torn out, Shiela."

Shiela let out a slow breath. "Nice."

"Animals don't . . . eat dead bodies, do they?"

"Won't hold up," Shiela protested. "Just when I begin to think my dog is human, he runs out in the yard and eats a gopher that's been dead for a week. Animals eat all kinds of crap, Lexey Jane. Sorry."

"But"—Lexey Jane held up a finger, looked around her, then leaned closer—"if a body is still alive, what is the first place an animal attacks?"

Shiela smiled thinly. "The throat."

"I have another name for you. Rudolph Hiatt."

"Lexey Jane!" Julian spluttered, "I told you not to talk to anyone else. I asked you to be a tourist, go sightseeing with a guide, stay in your room where you are safe!"

"And I did just that, Julien," she cooed. If she told him about the bathroom accident, he would send the militia. Besides, no need for him to know now. "Mr. Hiatt was Peaches' attorney here."

"Then can't you call him and ask . . . ?"

"He's dead."

A long pause. "Oh?"

"Julien?" She made her voice as cunning as possible. This would require delicacy. "Are you through in court?"

"Yes."

"Did you win?"

"Yes."

"That was a silly question, wasn't it?"

"Yes."

"Do you have time to take a trip?"

Silence.

"To Bordeaux, France?"

"Didn't you get the wine?"

"Yes."

"Then why do I need to go to Bordeaux!"

"I think there is some connection between those forged wine documents and our forged TC stock. And there's another peculiar link. There's a scientist in Bordeaux building a machine very similar to one that's being built here— outside Santa Fe."

"What machine is this?"

"Cosmic energy, or something. But crystals are involved, and I found out from one of Peaches' friends that she kept talking about crystals right before she died."

"I think we should just call this whole thing off. Since you've been in Santa Fe, two people have died."

"You make me sound like a plague." She laughed.

" . . . and I don't want anything to happen to you."

"Makes you a rich man faster, Julien."

"That is not funny!"

"I'm sorry, but Julien, there are too many similarities between Bordeaux and Santa Fe. Something is in the middle. I know it. Something that will help us trace that counterfeit certificate."

"I'm glad you remembered the problem."

"Now surely you have a contact in Bordeaux," she challenged.

He sighed helplessly. "I do know a physicist at the Medical Institute."

"Oh, Julien, that's excellent! Perhaps he can put you in touch with . . ."

"*She.*"

"Why, of course." Lexey Jane smiled. It always surprised her, this network of Julien's. She conjured up his face, his ruddy cheeks, blue-green eyes, slightly full jowls that filled with air when he spoke. And for the life of her she could not understand his desirability to women. Yet he had it. Quite definitely. She admired his mind, but sensually she found him about as exciting as dried toast. "Well, I'm sure she will come up with some information that will be valuable to us both." She tried to sound very businesslike.

"If I'm going to Bordeaux for you, would you do something for me?"

"Of course."

"Will you please stay inside the hotel until I'm back?"

"Of course, Julien," she replied charmingly. But her fingers were crossed.

She sat in the lobby of the La Fonda, watching the little charades between people passing back and forth. The engaging noise of the lobby reverberated off the tile floor and adobe walls. It flowed around her with a flamboyant excitement full of mirth, activity, good nature—all of which put her extremely out of sorts.

Why is it, she thought, that every time Julien asks me to stay in one place I feel more spry than ever. My bones stop aching and my feet itch. Ah, the ailments of a rebel, Lexey Jane. And you contracted that disease early in life. Boycotted the cotillion, remember? To the horror of every debutante friend, ran an ad in the paper saying the cotillion was a shallow show of affectation, a waste of money while others are starving and unemployed. Well, you learned a lesson from that, didn't you? Noblesse oblige. Threatened to put every waiter and caterer and musician and dressmaker and shopkeeper in the vicinity into a state of apoplexy. They all made six months' wages off that annual cotillion. The ironies of economics!

She smiled and looked down at the Delman shoes that wrapped softly around her old feet. She'd learned something else in the ensuing years. That wealth was not all that bad. It did bring certain comforts. Especially to bunions.

She leaned back and watched the Indians parade around the lobby. And the hippies with—no doubt—sizable trust funds somewhere back East, playing a game of poverty in their patched and ragged jeans as they ordered expensive meals in the restaurant off the lobby. She smiled again, understanding their failing.

She was not really thinking anything as she studied the

painting on one of the four-foot-thick pillars near her. It was a poster-painting of the Zuni's giant messenger Shalako. An Indian stood dwarfed at his side, gazing into the distant mountains. The enormous Shalako was covered in a feathered headdress, and had strange, flat lips which protruded like a bird's beak. But what caught Lexey Jane's eye was the feathered staff he carried. "I wonder what Julien would think if I came back with one of those." The thought made her laugh.

Suddenly, her head jerked back up. Shalako. The *messenger!* Oh, Lexey Jane, how could you have been so stupid!

You fool. Now you know where you saw the girl in Mannie's painting. Isis! Otherwise known as Iris. Iris, the *messenger* of Jupiter.

She hummed to herself, making little shifting rhythmic motions of satisfaction. "And Iris, says Homer, shoots straight through the skies with the ease of a terrified dove." Iris, walking the bend of a rainbow. Right across the front of a Transcontinental Communications stock certificate. Iris, leaping through the air over blades of grass reflecting all the colors of the spectrum.

Oh, Mannie! How clever of you!

Chapter Seven

It was raining. His feet still hurt. The flight from Paris had made him nauseous. Julien stood in the open door of the airport breathing in the damp, cool air. He pulled the collar of his raincoat up and smiled; it reminded him of how James Bond this whole thing was. He frowned. James Bond or not, the counterfeit was real. And so was his integrity and reputation.

He felt the slip of paper in his pocket with the meager information Kathryn Wyler had supplied. He took it out and read it again. "Rudolph Hiatt, second cousin to Peaches Lamberton Mueller, last address: Box 69 Bordeaux. Head of guerrilla operations, Western Zone, WW II."

He shoved it back in his pocket and hunched his shoulders. "Long shot," he muttered. "I am reduced to chasing a gnat halfway across the world, hoping I can catch a fly." He shivered and plunged into the sea of umbrellas to hail a taxi.

The steady downpour made it impossible to see any of the city, so he leaned back and folded in with his own miserable thoughts. "Here I am in the country that invented a machine to pull on your socks and boots, that designed the first musical typewriter, and shoes with little taillights on them for nightwalking. Maybe there *is* a connection between France and New Mexico. Well, at least I'll get to see Colette."

He'd met Colette when she was a child. Before his death, her father had been dean of the Bordeaux University of Law, and Julien had visited their home often, watching the beautiful child with less than puritanical thoughts. She'd tempted him like some nymphet Lolita and then suddenly hid herself beneath a lab smock and a hairnet. He wanted to remind her that she was a woman. But then, it was ungentlemanly to take advantage of an innocent temptress. Wasn't it?

A half-hour later, the driver pulled up to a dreary huddle of buildings. *Institut National de la Santé et de la Recherche Médicale.* Julien stepped disdainfully through the mud. It sucked at his shoes with every step. Inside, the waiting room was dark as dusk.

"Dr. Colette Ricarde, *s'il vous plaît*," he told the receptionist hidden in a shadow behind a desk.

"On peut demander le nom de Monsieur?"

"Julien Strauss."

In a moment she was back. *"Si Monsieur me suivera . . ."*

He followed her down a long, dark corridor. Colette stood behind a desk in a small cube of an office. "Julien! I did not believe when she told me who wanted to see me!"

"You didn't get my telegram?"

"No. But it is better this way. Such a surprise." Her hands darted through the air like startled birds.

Julien smiled at the slim young girl buried beneath the white smock who had forgotten she was beautiful. It only lent her more charm. Her long, dark hair was parted in the middle and knotted loosely in the back. Dark eyes in a porcelain face.

"Why?" She searched for her English. "What brings you to Bordeaux?"

"You. I came to take you to dinner. And shopping tomorrow."

"Ah," she laughed. "The American liberates France once more."

"No. Just one beautiful French woman."

She closed her eyes and breathed deeply as if smelling a perfume. When she opened them, she looked out the smudged window. "Why is it raining? Remember? At Reserve Etche Ona that day we drove to Bourguailh? The lunch in the garden?"

Julien reached across the desk to take her hand. "The food at the Splendid is just as good."

But she suddenly clasped her hands in front of her in exaggerated agony. "Oh, Julien! I don't know what I am saying. I am in the middle of a difficult experiment. It must be checked every twelve minutes." She glanced irritably at her large, bulky watch.

"Get an assistant to do it."

She smiled. It began slowly, then spread over her face. "You are a rogue. You want to halt medical science."

"On the contrary. I am here to learn about it."

Colette sat across from him, her cheeks reflecting the soft burgundy of a new dress. In the taxi, Julien had loosened her hair and now it tumbled over her shoulders. She held her glass of wine out to him. "You make me feel"—she giggled—"like a woman."

"That's good. That's what you are. And a very lovely one."

She looked out the window at the eighteenth-century city below, shimmering in the rain. "I forget sometimes." A small crease formed between her brows. "You said you wanted to find out about some research being done here in Bordeaux?"

"Do you know anything about a man named Antoine Herrault and a machine he's building?"

Her shoulders dropped. "What is the matter now?"

"I don't understand."

"Julien, Antoine is so . . . how do you say? Surrounded by scandal. I shiver when you ask me about him and his work."

"You know him?"

"Everyone in Bordeaux knows him."

"Then have another sip of wine, and tell me about Herrault."

"Where do I begin?" She looked out the window again. "First, he has very little formal education, so no one believes him. He was a radar technician in the Italian navy during the war. Then he was taken prisoner by the Germans. He escaped in 1943 and came here to work in the *Résistance*. After the war, he stayed. But"—her eyes flashed defiantly—"I say sometimes education does not matter. It is like . . . like the soil of Bordeaux." Her hand swept out toward the window and the lights of the city. "It is stony and poor, yet we grow the finest grapes in the world. Because the grape draws from the sun and not from the earth. That is what Antoine is doing!"

Julien reached across and squeezed her hand. "I believe you," he said softly. "Tell me something about the machine."

Her eyes brightened. "I can take you to see it tomorrow."

Julien looked into the dark brown pupils flecked with green. Colette's sudden entré to Herrault was going to shorten his trip. And right now he wasn't sure at all he wanted to hurry back to New York.

"Excellent. But you should prepare me just a little."

She sighed despondently again. "It is very expensive. All Bordeaux complains they cannot turn on their lights because Antoine's machine burns up all the electricity." She shrugged her shoulders, "But I say it is worth it, for a machine that will cure cancer."

"How expensive is it?"

"I hear many figures. But the last is three million dollars."

Julien pondered this. "Where does the money come from?"

"Julien!" She looked shocked. "It has been in all the papers."

"Not in the United States."

"It comes from the University here, some from the World Health Organization, and . . . and the government."

The moment Colette faltered, there was an imperceptible twitch in the corner of Julien's eye.

"Who in the government has supported him?"

"Jacques Duplessis," she murmured.

Calmly, Julien asked, "The same Jacques Duplessis who was deputy prime-minister, and ran for president, but was defeated, I believe." Not a flicker passed over Julien's face, but inside he could feel his pulse speeding. The same Jacques Duplessis who tried to shield the conspirators who forged the wine documents. The very same Jacques Duplessis who had been active in the French Resistance and just might know an excellent counterfeiter and a former OSS man.

This time Julien allowed himself a smile. The French and their underground. It was more of an international club than the Mafia.

"I can take you to see the machine," Colette went on, "but please be kind to Antoine. He has suffered so much."

"In what way?"

"To tell you all, Julien, would take days. But for an example. The Academy organized a committee of ten professors of science and medicine, an air force general, the chief legal officer of Bordeaux, the prefect of the province, an electronics expert, the dean of the Law School and five security experts. All to watch his experiments. They put special seals on the laboratory doors which were broken twice a day to check the mice, then replaced by security officers. Antoine would have had to use magic to switch the mice! And they still called him a fraud!"

Julien filled her glass. They were on their second bottle of Chateau Paveil '66, and Colette's flushed cheeks matcher her dress.

"Why is he so suspect?"

"Because he won't tell them how the machine works!" She leaned forward in a whisper. "I think it is probably a very simple thing, but Antoine knows such a simple cure for cancer would never be accepted, so he has built this large machine to conceal a very small thing."

"Who would not accept a cure for cancer with open arms?"

Colette's dark eyes swept the room in disgust. "The cancer cartel," she answered. "A very exclusive international club."

"And the membership?"

"Doctors and scientists from the best universities and medical schools—the ones who get millions of dollars in funding. Julien, more money is spent on cancer research than any one project in the world right now. And finding that cure has become . . . ah . . . a big business. If they admit that Antoine's machine might be a way to cure some kinds of cancer, then their big business is *fini*, finished."

Julien nodded. No need to believe that medicine was any different from General Motors. When large sums of money were involved, it all operated on the same level. Desperation and fear. He flinched. A pain sped through his right foot. *You ought to know, Julien Strauss. A large sum of money and the same two emotions have made you run clear to France.*

"I remember what a Nobel scientist said once," Colette went on, "that 'cancer is not a disease for which we will suffer a cure joyfully.' He was right."

He reached across and took her fingers lightly, drawing them to him and kissing the tips. "I cannot set the world right for you, Colette. I can only work on a small part of it. That's why I'd like to meet this Antoine Herrault. At the moment, it's my world that needs to be turned right side up. And he might have a clue as to how it can be done."

The next morning, the sun crept over the vineyards that sprawled in a wide horseshoe around the city, then blazed down into the Place de la Comédie in the heart of Bordeaux. Julien opened his window and inhaled deeply. The musty odor rising from the sun-steamed buildings, the sour scent of fermenting grapes, the damp coolness of the Garonne River all blended into a bouquet that far surpassed the wine bottled near the waterfront. Below, he saw Colette park her mud-splattered Peugeot. He smiled as she walked across the street to the hotel. The bright floral dress he'd bought her yesterday wrapped around her slender legs. Her hair was loose, tied back with a sheer scarf that fluttered behind her.

"You look lovely," he told her as they drove down the street.

She smiled, her teeth pressed against her upper lip, a memory of Gene Tierney. "Say it again." She laughed.

"You look lovely."

"I forget sometimes how much fun it is to be a woman."

The car crept through the early morning traffic, winding in and out of streets for what seemed endless miles. At last Colette pulled up in front of a dilapidated building in an ancient, crumbling district. "This is it?" Julien asked, surprised.

"Yes. It is his home. That was one of Antoine's specifications. That he build the machine in his home."

A door opened, and two children burst from it, laughing and running out into the sun. A young woman stood in the entrance. "This is Madame Herrault," Colette introduced him.

The young woman looked at the children flying into the rain-soaked garden near the street, mud already up to their ankles. She shook her head. *"Je ne sais pas . . . je ne sais pas."*

Julien stepped inside and was blinded on the spot. White. The room was dazzling, luminescent white. Sun streamed through the windows and danced off the fluid white plastic chairs, the solid white wooden tables, the white porcelain lamps. He didn't like it. He felt suddenly weak and drained. From somewhere he heard Colette say, "Antoine, this is a dear friend of mine from America. I told him about your machine and he wants to see it."

A short, stocky man in a sterile lab smock over a suit was already pulling him down a long corridor. *"Oui, oui."* He smiled broadly at Julien.

Julien trotted uncertainly to keep up with the scientist's exuberant stride. He could hear the air whining as they passed room after empty room, each one gleaming white. His heels clicked against the hard white tile.

"Oh, your watch!" Colette called out.

Julien slipped it off and laid it on a table before stepping into a large room. The four walls vibrated around him, alive with controls and knobs and flashing lights, switches, and coils. But the stumpy Frenchman was leaping toward still another room. They stepped down and entered a humming forest of generators and instruments. And a glass tube. Julien shook his head, trying to toss away the high, piercing, tick-ticking inside his eardrums.

Down more stairs. Another room. Julien caught his breath. In the place of honor, centered on the ceiling like a chandelier from "Star Trek," hung a five-ton, bell-shaped dome painted a brilliant orange. He felt something pulling, tugging at him like a magnet. The hair on his wrists quivered on his skin.

Colette smiled like a shy, pleased child. "It's all right. You can look up inside. It's safe."

Julien peered up into the eye of the immense dome. He could see a glass tube inside, the end of the tube he'd just seen in the room above, through which the so-called healing rays emanated. So this is IT. The magic lamp. He stepped back and viewed the enormousness of the structure. Take quite a few Aladdins to give this thing a good dusting, he huffed to himself. He glanced at Colette. "Orange?"

"That's the color of radiant energy."

He bit the corner of his mouth to hold back a smirk.

Antoine was hopping about the room shouting to him in French.

"Crystals," Julien tried to insert. "Are there crystals used in this machine?"

In midsentence, the short Frenchman pirouetted on his small feet and grabbed Julien's arm, pulling him down other hallways, corridors and doorways that opened from every nightmarish direction.

"Crystals," Julien repeated.

"Oil to cool the machine." Antoine thrust a finger at long hoses coiled like entrails, over the walls, hanging from ceilings, snaking along the baseboards.

"Le cristal!" Julien shouted.

"Not finished yet." Antoine smiled enigmatically. "You must come back soon . . . soon, I hope. When it is finished."

Bewildered, his body dazed, Julien stood outside the front door wondering how he got there. He blinked at the two small children near the street, now glistening dark with mud. Behind him, he heard Colette say goodbye to Herrault.

"Wait a minute!" He turned and drew himself to his full height until he was looking down at the thinning spot on top of the scientist's head. "Monsieur Herrault, do you . . . did you know a man named Rudolph Hiatt? Perhaps in the underground during the war?" Instinctively, he reached for the sleeve of the white smock to keep this whirling dervish from disappearing.

Antoine frowned, then smiled apologetically. "So many people help me in those times. I do not remember names." The white door closed in front of him.

Julien took a deep gulp of air. "It's *outré*," he said to Colette as they got back in the car. "Occult," he murmured.

"I imagine people said the same thing to Galileo." She
smiled coldly.

"Galileo wasn't financed by the French government and
the World Health Fund."

Colette glowered at the traffic, then settled into glum silence for the long trip back to the hotel.

"Colette." Julien stroked the back of her neck. "Could
you arrange for me to see Jacques Duplessis?"

Without looking at him, her face grew dark. "What are
you after, Julien? Did the British send you?"

"The British?"

She ignored the genuine puzzlement in his voice. "Yes.
The British. It wouldn't be the first time they've sent someone to spy on Antoine, try to trick him some way so they
can expose him as a fraud."

Julien slid his arm across her shoulders. "Colette, I
promise you the British did not send me. I am trying to
trace some stock certificates. Stock that I believe may have
belonged to a man named Rudolph Hiatt."

Gratefully, Colette grabbed his other hand. "Oh, chéri!"
Her fingers felt the smooth wrist. "Your watch. You forgot
it."

He lifted the dark hair from the back of her neck and
kissed her. "So *that's* Antoine's little trick." He chuckled
softly in her ear.

"I'll take it." Lexey Jane slid her fingers over the green
Cerrillos turquoise eyes, felt the silky serpent's head in her
palm. "Olive wood, you say. Perfect." She tapped the fe-
rule on the floor of Ortega's Gift Shop. "Nice sound."

The clerk looked up from the cash register, gave a small "another crazy tourist" shake of her head, and handed Lexey Jane her change.

In her room, Lexey Jane opened the telegram from Paris.

HAVE BEEN TO ATLANTIS.

She laughed aloud. Julien's sense of humor was improving. It was signed "Spock."

Next she called information for Mannie's number. "Now is that Ringer on . . . ?"

"Five-nineteen Palace," the operator answered.

"Thank you." She leaned back on the bed. It would be better not to face him on his home ground. Wasn't that the advice of advocates? If you cannot meet in your own territory, choose a neutral place. A place so packed with people it would be impossible to escape.

"Mannie? This is Lexey Jane. Why don't I treat you to lunch at the Palace Restaurant?"

"Sounds great. Say, I bought an old pickup yesterday. Going to start work on my house. Could I give you a lift?"

"Thank you, Mannie. But it's only two blocks away. And the doctor says I must walk as much as possible." She hung up, feeling foxy. There. She'd rendered herself a frail old lady. Good for a starter.

She could hear the brisk taps of her new cane on the brick as she crossed the plaza square. It tatted with the eagerness of a war drum. She smiled at the beautiful day. Beneath the portal of the Palace of Governors, the Indians were lined up on their blankets. Tourists crouched around them in thick huddles. She turned the corner and saw the restaurant a short distance away. Good choice, she thought. The legislative session had run over, and the place was full of government workers, senators, and representatives, lobbyists and shoppers.

Inside, she surveyed her troops. Crowds of people mustered around small tables, platoons of tourists crushed into booths, a regiment stood along the bar and lined the small foyer. "Perfect." She smiled, and inched her way toward the booth she had reserved in the far corner beneath a canopy. Someone in the bar was playing the piano. She began to smile. It became a chuckle. They were playing "It Had to Be You," and Mannie was walking in the door, squinting in the dim light.

Now stop it, she warned herself. You're being entirely too flippant about this. She tried to straightened her face, but the best she.could manage was a smug smile. "Hello, Mannie."

"It's swarming in here!" He scooted beside her. "What's going on?" He looked out over the mass of diners, the chatter, the clink of silver.

"Legislature's still in session and the word is that they serve the best green chili cheeseburger in town."

"How about a drink first?"

"Splendid."

"I'll have a scotch and water," Mannie told the waitress, "and warm gin for the lady."

The waitress' eyes fluttered to the ceiling. "Warm gin?"

"No ice," Lexey Jane clarified.

As if this had restored sanity to the request, the waitress sighed in relief. "Oh." In a moment she was back.

"Well, Mannie." Lexey Jane raised her glass. "Let's drink a toast."

"I'm for that."

"To Iris."

"To—" Mannie held his glass in the air, staring at her over the rim. "Who is Iris?"

"Why, the girl in the painting, of course."

A tiny flicker of puzzlement scattered over his face. "Of course," he mumbled.

"And the girl on the front of a Transcontinental Communications certificate." She was truly enjoying herself! That was not nice at all.

The color drained from Mannie's face. The scars stood out. His eyes darted wildly around the room for a second. When he looked back at Lexey Jane, he was smiling at her. "What are you talking about?"

"You know very well what I'm talking about, Emmanuel Ringer."

"Sorry." He turned the glass in his hand. "I don't."

"I happen to own some TC stock with the same serial numbers as those you made."

His face broke into a frosty grin. He fumbled with his nose. "Is this some kind of a joke?"

His charade was beginning to irritate her. Too late for stealth and cunning. "Now Mannie, it will all be quite simple if you will just admit that you are the counterfeiter."

He gave a discordant laugh. "Look, I don't know what you're after, but I'm not going to play this little game. If you want to be a detective, do it with someone else."

Maybe she should have had Shiela come along. Perhaps Frank Parcher would have been a better match for him. "I need help," she said, "and in return for that help I can get you a suspended sentence."

"What?"

"But don't you see?" she persisted, "if you help me, I can help you in return. I can make it easier for you. I . . . I have some very valuable contacts with galleries."

Mannie bit his lip. His beard jutted out. "Okay, I'll play your game. Let's pretend I am that counterfeiter you're looking for. Now"—he gave a mock bow—"what can I do for you?"

Lexey Jane considered his question a moment. Can't tell him I need him to show us which stocks are real. Then he would really laugh. Have to catch him first. "A woman has lost her life, perhaps been murdered because of that certificate. You could help, Mannie. Help me find the murderer. And I will do everything I can to help you become the kind of artist you want to be. And your past will not keep rising up to haunt you. Think of it, Mannie. A clean slate." Lexey Jane's eyes danced with challenge.

He looked at her steadily. "I have nothing to apologize for."

"Mannie, I could make your name as well known as Manet, Degas, or Renoir." Oh dear, she thought. Julien would put that statement in the dirty tricks department.

He studied her for a long time. Lexey Jane shivered. It was the unblinking stare of the snake on the head of her new cane. Then, suddenly his shoulders slumped forward. And she was sorry. Sorry that she'd approached this with such swagger. After all, she was dealing with a life, a life all full of dreams and hopes.

"Okay. What if I did counterfeit those stocks? Then how could I help you find this murderer?"

"You could tell me who contracted you to make that certificate."

He gave a burlesque shrug. "But I don't know. Do you want me to make up a name?"

"Was it a man?" she asked sharply.

"Could have been."

"What did he say? Did he tell you why he wanted them?"

"Well, now, let's see . . . what would he have told me?" He jerked his head toward her, puzzled. "Lexey Jane? Who the hell *is* Iris?"

"A Greek goddess." She smiled. "A messenger for Jupiter."

Mannie rubbed a hand over his beard. She could see paint caught beneath his fingernails. He is really trying, she thought. He is really trying to be honest. "Could you tell me what he looked like? Did you see him? Meet with him?"

"Oh," he answered her, suave and convincing, "I don't think I would do it that way at all. I mean, if I were a counterfeiter, I'd never let anyone see me. I'd do it all over the phone. A pay phone. Isn't that what they use in the movies? And then I'd deliver the finished product to . . . let's see . . . a public place. Like a post office box." He grinned at her.

"Could he have seen you? When you delivered them to the box?"

"Oh, sure, that's possible. Anything's possible, isn't it?"

She flinched as if she'd been shot with her own weapon.

The whole thing was going wrong. He was acting monstrously absurd. "This is serious, Mannie."

"Oh, I can see that it is." He smiled into his drink.

"Do you remember anything about his voice over the phone? What it sounded like?"

"Now, let's see." He gazed out over the heads in the dining room. "If I were a counterfeiter and I had done a job for someone in Santa Fe, I can bet you it would be for one of those joggers running up and down the roads all the time. So he'd be all out of breath." He began to pant like a buffoon.

"You are not making this easy."

His eyes flared. "Oh? I'm so sorry."

"You did deliver the stocks here. And you liked Santa Fe so well, you decided to set up residence," she guessed. "And that nasty lie at the Lamy station about no telephone up at that restaurant. You just didn't want to leave that precious suitcase, did you? And you didn't want to lug the heavy thing up the hill."

Mannie grinned gamely at her.

"You had something valuable in that suitcase, didn't you?"

"Sure. Packed full of hundred-dollar bills—all counterfeit." He gave a disgusted laugh.

"Perhaps steel-engraved plates, your tools? Work that was so expert you could not bear to destroy it. Mannie, you are a forger of unmatched talent."

He took a long gulp of his drink.

"I don't know how to ask you without being tactless . . ."

"Hasn't bothered you so far."

Lexey Jane bit her lip. "Did you murder Peaches Mueller?"

He looked straight at her. "You're right. That is pretty tactless. No. I did not."

"Well," she sighed, "let's order one of those green chili things."

"Good idea. This is getting boring." He raised his finger for a waitress.

"Mannie, how did that man get in touch with you? How did he know your profession?" She shot it at him, "Bordeaux, France, perhaps?"

He went white. "What the . . . ?" He whirled on her.

"The forged wine documents." She reached out and touched his wristwatch. "You have been in Europe, Mannie. Only place you can buy one of those."

"How do you know it wasn't a gift?"

"I don't."

"Sure, I've been in Europe. If you want to put me in prison for that, I'm going to have lots of company. What are you? A secret agent for Bulova?"

She laid her hand gently on his arm. "Mannie. You did admit it."

"What?"

"That you are the counterfeiter."

A broad, derisive grin crisscrossed his face. "No, Lexey Jane. I didn't."

Chapter Eight

Julien gazed out the window as Colette drove him to the airport. In the distance he could see workers on the hillsides pruning back the vines, readying them for the next crop. Overhead, a helicopter whirred low like a giant praying mantis, spraying the vineyards against fungus. Colette was quiet. He leaned back to think.

The meeting with Duplessis had been cordial and brisk. Despite the man's balding head and slight paunch, he had that innate, imposing eloquence which only certain French politicians are able to carry off. A bearing that exuded a Louis XVI brocade, gilt, and fine marble. In fact, Duplessis had surrounded himself with eighteenth-century furnishings.

Julien had quickly noted the Joubert copy of a flat-topped desk which, no doubt, lacked the forty-two coats of scarlet lacquer to give it the desired patina. But the Chinese figures painted in gold were an impressive duplication.

Next to a fine rendition of a Criaerd chair was a small Boulle table with an ebony and ivory marquetry inlay. Near the door, a splendid facsimile of a Gaudreaux chest. Against one wall, an excellent copy of a Riesener cabinet with the counterpart of a Lépine clock on top. Julien had smiled to himself; the room was so appropriate to the matter at hand. Forgeries of furniture of the "high period" were in plentiful supply. But Duplessis had chosen only those with an unmatched level of craftsmanship. The Versailles staff would have been pleased.

"I am looking for a man named Rudolph Hiatt," Julien had told him. "Mademoiselle Ricarde thought perhaps you might be of help."

"*Oui, oui,* I know Monsieur Hiatt. He is missing, you say?"

At that moment a silver tray was brought in carrying a decanter and two glasses. Deftly, Duplessis poured himself a taste, rolled the amber liquid around the glass, then sipped it. Next he poured Julien's glass. Three sips full. Amused, Julien moved it in his hand. Duplessis had filled his own glass to the brim. Evidently, he must have touched upon a delicate subject, and Duplessis wanted the meeting to be brief.

Julien tasted the claret. No. He stopped the thought. It was unthinkable. The furniture perhaps . . . the documents . . . the certificate . . . but not the wine.

"He is . . . uh . . . *in transitu,* so to speak. And I have an important message for him."

"Ah." Duplessis had walked to the window and gazed out. "Well, I have not seen Monsieur Hiatt for . . . for over one year. We were friends in the underground during the war." He turned and smiled coolly at Julien. "Monsieur

Hiatt is a great patriot." The smile folded back into Duplessis' jowls with a deadly, menacing twist. "Between us, we
killed many Germans."

The claret stuck in Julien's throat. He felt it rise into his
nose, choking him. His throat tightened, trying to strangle
the cough.

"Uh . . . several years ago, there were wine documents
forged here in Bordeaux." Julien looked at him steadily.
"Did you ever apprehend the forger?" *Touché!*

Duplessis picked up a silver letter-opener from his desk
and ran it back and forth between his fingers. "No."

What was it? From the first mention of Rudolph Hiatt's
name, the room had become forboding, sinister. Duplessis
stood across the office, sliding that damned knife back and
forth in his hand, his head cocked slyly at Julien, as if wondering whether it was too late to kill one more German for
the glory of France.

"I have read in the papers that you've been instrumental
in getting money for Antoine Herrault."

Duplessis gave a slight nod. "I have done what I could for
the progress of medical science."

"Do you really believe this . . . this machine of his can
cure cancer?"

The Frenchman shrugged. "Who knows, monsieur. I
support his research out of love for mankind."

"Whoever comes up with a cure for cancer stands to
make millions. Even if it is a hoax." Julien watched him
carefully above the rim of his glass. He saw the creases
around Duplessis' mouth whiten.

"Ah, yes." He nodded again. "I remember how much
money was made with the Salk vaccine. But, we don't have
polio anymore, do we, Monsieur . . . ah . . . ?"

"Strauss. Julien Strauss."

"Ah, yes. Strauss." He spat the word, slapping the letter-opener against his palm.

Julien downed his third and last sip of the claret. Damned underground. Damned French resistance. So many of them were still living in a lost moment of sentimental brutality. Suddenly, something froze his spine.

The Lépine clock struck two notes. His feet stopped hurting. "Handsome copy." Julien smiled unctuously, glancing at the clock.

The letter-opener halted in midair. "You have an experienced eye, Monsieur Strauss."

"Very." Julien set his glass on the tray with certainty, then looked triumphantly at Duplessis. The obliqueness of the French, he smiled to himself. We could discuss Louis XVI imitations all afternoon, and we would still be talking about counterfeit stocks. He rose to go.

Duplessis seemed relieved. "I am afraid I am not much help to you." His lips puckered soulfully.

Julien set his empty glass on the table. He glanced around the room once more. The decor might be artificial, but the danger—wherever it was—was real. He had to get Lexey Jane out of that place. "On the contrary. You have been of great help." He left Duplessis frowning at the ornate clock.

No confessions, he thought, looking across at Colette as she maneuvered through the traffic. But the circumstantial evidence was thick. I may have caught myself a fly after all. He reached over and twisted her hair around his fingers as she drove, knowing within the hour it would be wound into a bun again.

"*Chéri,* I brought these for you to read." Colette parked

at the airport and reached into the back seat. She handed Julien a thick stack of papers. "These are reports on Antoine's machine, experiments . . ." She leafed through them. "A paper presented before the French Academy of Science, a British study, and"—she smiled coyly at him—"a study done at Columbia University on electromagnetic fields."

Julien gathered the papers under his arm. "*Chéri,* please don't laugh," she begged him, "it is very serious work."

"Even a skeptic keeps a window half-open." He leaned down and kissed her.

"*Merci,*" she whispered, "*merci mille fois.* Please come back. You are much nicer than white mice." She smiled.

"When I forget how lovely you are, I'll be back."

Lexey Jane wandered slowly back to the hotel, trying to unscramble her thoughts and feelings. Her cane thumped out a dirge on the pavement.

She had mistakenly hoped she could bribe Mannie, appeal to his pentup, frustrated dreams, his confidence in his unique talent.

Lexey Jane stopped in front of a blanket draped with heishi necklaces, round shells rolled and rolled against stone until they were tiny, slender beads. "I handled it so badly," she mumbled aloud.

"Forty-two dollars."

Startled, she looked down into a round, cinnamon-colored face peering out of a blanket. "Oh. Thank you." She quickly paid the Indian and dropped the necklace into her purse. *I must stop talking to myself.*

She paused again in front of some turquoise belt buckles and bolo ties. "I should get Julien something."

At the thought of Julien, she sank. She had been so stupid with Mannie that now she might lose him. And that would not make Julien happy at all.

She tapped her cane hard in front of a belt buckle.

He knows his work is good. He knows that without him I cannot tell which is the real stock and which is the counterfeit. But he did *not* admit he was the counterfeiter, Lexey Jane. But of course he is. I know it. I just know it.

She tapped again. Below her, a hand scrambled back and forth over the display, trying to follow the direction of the cane.

Well, he's not going to help. That is a truth you must face. That was Plan A and it's been set aside temporarily. Time to move to Plan B. Find this Dr. Filiamo.

With new confidence, she banged her cane on the walk.

"Lady!" She heard a voice calling after her. A corpulent Indian was handing her a brown-wrapped package. "One hundred fifty dollars." He smiled.

"Oh dear." She fumbled in her purse. "I must stop talking to myself." She took the package. "I hope it's the real thing."

"It is. It is," the Indian assured her. "No fake crap sold here."

She counted out the money. "Damn!" Her fingers halted on a dollar bill. The Great Seal of the United States jumped out at her—an encircled pyramid. And above it hung the capstone, bathed in light, an eye gazing with omnipotent indifference from its center. "It's all around me," she complained to the bewildered Indian. "Even in my pocket!"

The manager at the desk smiled down at her benignly. "Shiela McCarthy? She should be back shortly. Why don't you wait in the lobby for her."

Within fifteen minutes, Shiela was standing in front of her, completely shrouded in a cape and hood.

"Let me buy you a drink. You look terrible." Lexey Jane frowned.

"I need one."

"What is it? What's happening to you?" Lexey Jane leaned across the table. But Shiela only shook her head, rubbing her face in her hands. She looked up at Lexey Jane with swollen eyes. "Have you found out anything else?"

"Shiela, have you heard of a man called Dr. Filiamo?"

"Here in Santa Fe?"

"Somewhere around here, I think. Up in the mountains, perhaps."

"What does he do?"

"He's a scientist of sorts, working on a machine to cure cancer. A machine that uses crystals. I think that's where the money went. The money Peaches paid for the TC stock."

Shiela's mouth twisted. "Lexey Jane, are you certain Mrs. Mueller spent that million?"

"Well . . . we have the stock to prove it. Why?"

Shiela leaned back in the chair. "I think I better tell you that Mrs. Mueller spent that million dollars so many times it was as shredded as coleslaw."

"What?"

"I mean she *promised* to spend it." She gave a short, bitter laugh. "She even promised to loan it to me. She was a liar. A pathological liar. When I went to her for weaving lessons I was in a pretty vulnerable state. She was kind and concerned, so finally I told her about my problems, and she said she would loan me a million dollars. I just thanked her. Lexey Jane"—Shiela smiled dismally—"Mrs. Mueller offered that million dollars every time she thought it would put her in someone's good graces. Every time she wanted someone to love her. But she never really gave it to anyone. I don't believe she even had the money."

These revelations about Peaches saddened Lexey Jane. She must remember that Peaches had been a good friend to her. And she knew the million existed. "It does not change the problem, Shiela. We've got a counterfeit certificate that could tear up a world corporation."

"How do you think this scientist could help?"

"I feel he might help me pin down the counterfeiter." She pressed her thumb against the table. If Mannie would not cooperate, she would find another way.

"What's his name again?"

"Filiamo."

Shiela shook her head. "Strange. Santa Fe is a pretty small town. And you hear about the nuts first. But I've never heard his name. Maybe he lives on the Hill."

"The Hill?"

"Los Alamos, the atomic bomb, remember? It's about forty miles away. Where it all began and where it will all probably end." She sat up sharply. "Wait a minute! Fili . . . Fili . . ." The palm of her hand flew to her forehead. "I have a . . . friend who has talked about someone named Fili."

Lexey Jane leaned forward excitedly. "Could I talk to him?"

Shiela nodded grimly. "If you want to come to the hospital with me."

She opened the heavy door for Lexey Jane. Inside the room, she slumped against the wall. "That's all I have left in the world," she whispered.

In a hospital bed, behind a fence of metal bars, a young

boy lay spraddled on a white sheet. Tubes ran from both arms to standards beside the bed, dripping glucose into the thin sleeping body. His face was blue in the light, and his lips trembled with fever.

"Your son?"

"Devon. I'm afraid he can't help us now. They've just given him a sedative." Her voice rang flat against the chrome and metal.

Lexey Jane could scarcely speak. The pain inside her bones reverberated back and forth between her and the small figure on the bed.

"What is it?"

"The plague. The bubonic plague."

The word sounded strange in the modern hospital room, anachronistic, out of time, out of history. "But I thought . . ."

"You thought it was something you read about in history books and novels like *Forever Amber?* So did I. But it's common out here. The fleas on animals carry it. We thought it was the flu. His fever went up and down. Then the glands in his neck and armpits began to swell."

"We?"

"I . . . I thought it was the flu."

"Nothing out here is what it seems to be," Lexey Jane muttered.

Shiela jerked toward her. "I had to hide him. Before, Tim—my husband—borrowed some money, quite a lot of money. When the insurance policies wouldn't pay off, I got kidnapping threats. People thought I'd stashed away a fortune somewhere. Scared the hell out of me. So I hid Devon. Up in the mountains. Mrs. Mueller helped me find the place. That's what terrified me that day you found her dead. Some way I thought I'd caused that too."

"Oh, Shiela," Lexey Jane groaned against the agony that filled the room.

From beneath the folds of her cape, Shiela spread her small hands desperately. "Hilarious, isn't it? I come to the desert to hide and lick my wounds. I come to the desert and he gets a disease that belongs on wharfs and waterfronts." Her face pleaded with Lexey Jane. Tears ran down her cheeks.

Lexey Jane glanced again at the small, inert body. She knew the pain coursing through his bloodstream, through every organ, the muscles, through the marrow of his bones. The small blue face twitched. It was no time to ask about Filiamo.

As if Shiela had read her thoughts, she said, "When he first started running a fever, he would talk about 'Fili' as if it were a person. I don't know. Maybe I'm wrong. Maybe he was trying to say 'feel.' I guess Frank Parcher hopped to the forefront when you mentioned that name." She shook her head and then shuddered. "I guess I wanted you to know. How sick he is. I needed someone to share it with me."

"You're exhausted," Lexey Jane said gently. "Come back to the room with me and lie down for awhile. Rest. There's nothing you can do by sitting here hour after hour."

They drove back. Shiela left word at the desk and they rode up in silence. Lexey Jane opened her door. The latch clicked; immediately there was a second click, a sharp cocking sound. Annie Mueller was facing her in the chair pointing a pistol at her heart.

"What are you doing here?" Shiela screamed.

"The damned electricity went out again! I came into town to study!" Annie screamed back.

"I told you never to use that! I told you to throw it away!" Shiela pushed Lexey Jane aside, knocking her against the wall.

"Jerry makes me carry it when I go to work by myself!" Annie shouted. "Don't worry. I hide it when Devon's there." She dumped the gun into a large purse at her side. "I was only checking it," she grumbled.

Lexey Jane swallowed her relief. Then a slow prickling crept up her spine. Annie glowered at Lexey Jane with dark, animal eyes. "I didn't kill her."

Lexey Jane jumped. "Who?"

"Auntie Peaches. I didn't kill her."

"I . . . how . . . I . . . ?"

She turned on Shiela. "You told me she thought I'd killed her!" Annie half-rose out of the chair.

Shiela dropped on the bed and looked at Lexey Jane. "I told her you suspected her, and that I would straighten it out. I didn't know she was going to come here"—she glared at Annie—"with a gun."

"I wanted to kill her," Annie said flatly. She tossed her head at Shiela. "And so did you. God, how we both wanted to kill her. There were times when I hated her so much, I could have done it." Her eyes flicked back to Lexey Jane. "But I didn't."

The phone rang. All three of them leaped. It was for Shiela. She hung up and closed her eyes with fatigue. "A guest is at the bus station. I'll be back."

Lexey Jane sat on the edge of the bed. Annie looked at her, then away, then back again. "We kept Devon for her. That's where he got the flea bite." She clenched her teeth. "She thinks it's our fault. I know she's uptight, so I'm not arguing with her. But, damnit, he could have been bitten anywhere! It's one of the risks out here. You've got tornadoes in Oklahoma, hurricanes in Florida, earthquakes in California, and you've got the plague in New Mexico." She sighed heavily. "He'll be all right. With antibiotics, he'll be all right."

"I hope so," Lexey Jane answered. The tire swing hanging from the tree outside the pyramid—it had been for Devon. She looked at Annie, studying her, trying to see her as she was that afternoon, floating on the pillows in the center of the floor, radiant and beautiful. Now she looked as tired as Shiela. "Why did you hate Peaches so?"

"The money mostly." Annie ran a fingernail nervously along the crease of her faded jeans. "She'd hold it out to me, dangle it in front of me, tantalize me with it. Then she'd grab it back, saying it wasn't mine until I followed all her rules. I had to leave Jerry, for one. She was evil with that money. She knew how Jerry could spend it. She knew how hard I had to work to make ends meet. Sooo," Annie expelled a long sigh, "she'd wait until I'd had weeks of working out there at that damned restaurant, trying to make my classes at the college, until I'd had it up to here." The plam of her hand sliced her throat. "Then she'd call and ask me to come see her. Whining over the phone that I didn't love her—all that crap. When I showed up, feeling guilty as hell, she would bring up my inheritance again. And by that time, I was so exhausted I would have done just about anything for that money. Anything, but murder. I couldn't do that. The last time it happened"—her teeth tightened again—"I went up there and she was sitting at her loom. Never looked at me. Just sat there shoving that yarn through the threads, that steady clack, clack of the shuttle, and I thought I'd kill her right then! I ran home bawling and told Jerry I was going to strangle her."

"Or smother her?"

Annie frowned. "Oh." She smiled quickly. "Like Desdemona? Maybe that's what I said. I don't remember."

"What does Jerry spend the money on?"

Annie waved her hand in the air. "Generators, transformers, electrical equipment. It's all very expensive."

"What does he do with it?"

Annie looked at her. "You heard him. He's all wrapped up in this cosmic energy stuff, electromagnetic fields . . . I don't understand half of it."

Lexey Jane chewed the inside of her cheek. Careful. Careful, she cautioned herself. You mustn't sound like some righteous Rotarian. "Uh . . . Jerry . . . why can't he get a job? Help out a bit . . ."

Annie exploded. "Because he's working on those goddamned fool experiments all the time! And he keeps saying it's going to make us rich."

Lexey Jane smiled. "Even you sound a little irked with him. Why—I don't want to sound like Peaches—but why *don't* you leave him?"

Anne Mueller exhaled a long sigh and looked around the room. She twisted her fingers in her lap. When she glanced up, her eyes were rimmed with tears. "Because I love him."

Lexey Jane looked out the window above Annie's head, at the clouds scudding across the darkening sky. She could hear her husband Augustus wheezing about during his last days. "It's a trifle warm in here, don't you think?" "It's a trifle cold in here, don't you think?" And the huffing, puffing, "Yes, yes my dear . . ." His senility had filled the house, nettling her so she wanted to lace his tea with laudanum! But she didn't. Some super-power, some force, some ache deep inside a memory kept her wits fresh and strong. It was beyond all logic, all rationale. Only after the ambulance took him away was she able to give it words. "I loved him," she thought now, as she had that day.

"I understand," she whispered to the young girl across the room.

"The money's gone, isn't it?"

Lexey Jane nodded. "Yes."

"Shiela said it wasn't—that it never was there. But I knew it was. I wish I could help you find it."

Lexey Jane brightened. "Perhaps you can. Could you tell me where I can find this Dr. Filiamo?"

"Dr. Filiamo?"

"Yes. The man Jerry mentioned."

"Oh." Annie shook her head. "I think he's a figment of Jerry's overactive imagination."

"No, he gave me a magazine with an article in it about this doctor." She looked around the room. "Here it is." Lexey Jane handed her the copy of *Beyond.*

"Oh, that." Annie laughed. "Jerry gave me a subscription for Christmas. And it's a bunch of crap. I think someone makes up all the articles printed in there."

"Oh?" Possible. But how tragic. It's bad enough to sell hope for $49.95. But to sell false hope? "If a Dr. Filiamo exists, then you don't know where he is?"

Annie shook her head.

"But he's supposed to be around here. Around Santa Fe somewhere," she protested weakly.

Annie studied her. "Have you seen this evening's newspaper?"

Lexey Jane frowned. "No."

"Well, they found a plane up in the mountains yesterday. You know when that plane crashed? Seven years ago! And they've been looking for it ever since." She glanced at the wall as if beyond it she could see the arroyos, canyons, eroded hills with their endless hiding places, the mountains with their treacherous serenity. "If you think you can find this Dr. Filiamo up there, then good luck!"

"I'm sorry I blew up at Annie." Shiela took off the cape

and slumped into a chair. "I'm just tired. It was seeing that gun."

Lexey Jane handed her a sandwich she'd ordered. "Here. Eat. It makes all those molecules work on something other than memories."

Shiela managed a smile. "Thanks." She took a bite and chewed it slowly. "I'm glad you know about Devon."

"He's going to be all right," Lexey Jane answered. The magic words. The adult kiss on the skinned knee. For a moment, she was in Wilmington and had just found out her daughter Anne was dead. An arm was around her, her old housekeeper's arm smelling of soap and freshly ironed cotton, and she was saying, "Everything's going to be all right." The mantra of the human soul.

"Everything's going to be all right," she said softly.

"You know what he did." Shiela choked down the bite. Her saliva wouldn't work. "He shot himself in front of me. I walked into the bedroom and he was standing there with the dresser drawer open and he took the gun and looked at me and held it to his head . . . I tried to stop the blood. It was coming out everywhere . . . out his nose and eyes and mouth and ears . . . all those places I'd kissed and tasted with my tongue and loved . . ." Her chest heaved with a sob. "In front of me. I'll never understand. I'll never understand any of it."

"He wasn't himself then. You know that."

Shiela nodded. "I know. I know. I just wish I could cauterize that part of my brain. The part that remembers."

The surge of emotion had released all her exhaustion. Lexey Jane made her lie on the bed. In a moment she was asleep.

The phone rang and a man asked for Shiela. "She's asleep," Lexey Jane protested.

"I think you better wake her."

Reluctantly, Lexey Jane gently shook the thin shoulder. "Shiela, there's a phone call for you. They won't leave a message."

Groggily, Shiela took the receiver. Her eyes bolted open. "What?" She threw it across the bed. "He's gone! He's gone!" She leaped across the room. "Devon. He's gone from the hospital! He's not in his room—they can't find him!" She was running in the narrow space between the bed and chair, tearing at the spread, high, frightened animal sounds coming from her throat.

"Let me go with you!"

Shiela whirled on her as if she were an enemy. "No," she gasped, glancing at the cane, at the frail legs, "No. I can go faster by myself."

Lexey Jane looked at the door slamming behind Shiela. She slumped into the chair, then she tottered into the bathroom and splashed water on her face. "Why don't I feel inside as old as I am on the outside?" she asked her reflection. "Deception," she muttered to the folds of skin falling over her eyes. "Misleading," she grumbled to the spider web wrinkles around her lips. She threw the towel aside and shook her finger at the mirror. "Come to your senses, old girl. Your youth simply has a different look about it."

She called the hospital and was told in obsequious terms that Shiela McCarthy had left. No, they did not know anything about a patient disappearing. They were not able to give out that information. She left word for Shiela to call her, then hung up.

Lexey Jane looked at the small vial of pills on the bedside table. The pain, aggravated by tension, jagged through her with such intensity she winced. "No, I will not take one. I will lie back on the bed by the phone. I must be alert when she calls. She'll need my help."

At nine-thirty the phone blasted her eardrum. She jolted upright. Trembling, she grabbed for it. "Yes?"

"I'm sorry. I woke you."

"Oh, Julien. Yes, I . . . I guess I did doze off."

"I'm wide awake. Jet lag, I guess."

"Aren't you relieved to find me right where I'm supposed to be?"

"Yes, I am. And I want you out of there immediately."

"Something happened in Bordeaux. What was it?"

She waited through the hesitation. "I saw the machine. The one that's supposed to cure cancer and everything else that ails the human species," Julien answered at last.

"If it can cure cancer, then why . . . ?"

"It seems one of the reasons is the 'cancer cartel.'"

"What, in heaven's name, is that?"

Another silence. "Let me put it this way. Champallion was sixteen when he read his first paper before the Academy of Grenoble deciphering the Rosetta Stone. And a great number of scholars wanted to dig their own graves." Lexey Jane heard him give a little sniff of pleasure at the pun. "You see," he went on, "it was rather ego-crushing to have some mere child come up with the answers to the mystery of Egyptian hieroglyphics. I'm told the same opposition is working against Herrault. First of all, his machine is outside the familiar areas of cancer research—chemotherapy, viral studies, and the like—in fact, it's outside the areas of human comprehension."

Lexey Jane heard his voice rise.

"Anyway, the best doctors and scientists in the world are not about to give credence to a tinker who says he can cure cancer with a couple of horseshoe magnets."

"I see. This Frenchman does not belong to the club, in other words. That's tragic."

"No. It's big business. Also, they're an extremely cautious group. They deal in certainties, not hope."

"A shame. The world is in such need of it. Do you think this Herrault has something?"

"I was tracing the counterfeit stock, remember?"

"And . . . ?"

"I strongly suspect a link."

"Give me credit, Julien."

"Your suspicions may have foundation," he corrected. "The politician who has helped fund Herrault was also involved in protecting the men who were responsible for the wine scandal."

Lexey Jane heard the tightness in his voice. Whatever happened in Bordeaux, happened with the Frenchman.

" . . . he knew Rudolph Hiatt from the war. They were old friends from the resistance days."

"Doesn't sound like you cared for this Frenchman."

"Duplessis? He's a fraud. And most frauds deal in fraud."

"You think he's part of the puzzle then."

"I'm down to numbers again, Lexey Jane. If Mrs. Mueller, Hiatt, and this Duplessis are somehow connected, then the statistics are not good. Two out of three are dead. That's why I want you back here." She heard him huff commandingly. "I'm going to try to alarm you, Lexey Jane. You are in danger."

"Fiddlesticks! A counterfeiter doesn't go around murdering people, remember?"

"Someone does."

"Oh, Julien, it's so nice to have someone agree with me—that they were murdered."

"Lexey Jane!"

"Don't worry, Julien. You'll be a rich man."

She hung up and propped the pillow behind her head,

then dialed the hospital again. No, Shiela McCarthy was not in the building.

She closed her eyes. They popped back open. What a sad world, she thought. A man invents a machine that will cure cancer and no one will pay attention to him. But then you can't go around believing every crackpot that comes up with a cure for something, Lexey Jane! Be sensible. Still, wouldn't it be nice if you could hold a crystal over poor Devon McCarthy and make him well? Take away the pain? So he could jump up from that hospital bed and swing . . . but he's not in that hospital bed, Lexey Jane.

"Oh! Nothing is what it's supposed to be! Everything is upside down and out of place!"

She leaned back against the pillow, closed her eyes again. Suddenly, she bolted. "Of course!" she cried. Forgetting the pain in her bones, she scrambled across the bed for the paper sack. She dumped out the contents, shuffling through them quickly.

This time, she knew what she was looking for.

The bare overhead bulb in Mannie's studio swung in the air as he stepped back to get a distant look at his canvas. It reminded him that he would have to jack up the sagging floor. Or was it the scotch? He wasn't sure anymore.

He picked up the bottle from the wooden bench and gulped deeply. How can you think about the destruction of a dream that's come true. It's okay as long as it's in the making. He'd been thwarted before, again and again. That's all right if you're still dreaming the dream. But once it's there, in your clutch, you're living it, actually living it, then have it jerked out from under you!

He walked back across the tilting floor and applied a fine brushstroke. Squinting in the poor light, he leaned back to look at it again. It was a portrait of Lexey Jane. From memory, he had seated her in one of the wide chairs in the La Fonda lobby like some sovereign dowager, her back regally straight, her fingers curled over the white head of her cane. He'd captured the courage in the face, the tilt of the chin, even the twinkle in the eyes. "Agh!" He threw the brush on the floor in disgust.

Mannie Ringer had been trapped only once. He was a seventeen-year-old "paper hanger" dealing in bogus checks and the court had placed him in a detention home. Even now he could conjure up a shiver at the memory of closed gates, fences, constant surveillance. It was a tightness that gave claustrophobia to the soul. He had promised himself that he would never again view the world through a slit.

Since then, he had walked on eggshells to further his talent. He always worked through a contact. And even then, he never let his face be seen.

The fear had lived so long inside him, it was part of his corpuscles. So much that he'd even been afraid to leave that damned suitcase filled with engravings and steel plates and tools in the care of an old woman who couldn't have lifted the key to open it. It was the dread of being locked up, that terrifying memory of youth that forced him to work like a shadow, like some invisible man.

It had not been easy. His work was a masterpiece of carftsmanship, acknowledged as such by any Secret Service agent. He had buried himself for months, years, in the mysteries of engraving, inks, color registration, and printing. He gave his work such painstaking attention that often his time and materials cut deeply into his profit.

And no recognition. Sometimes it ate into him. If he could paint, sell his paintings, live without fear, like other people . . . what would that be like? I could be a famous painter, he would tell himself. The day will come. The day will come, he'd told himself for years. Until it became a kind of motto. THE DAY WILL COME.

It came. The call from Bordeaux. A contact from his job on the wine documents. He had hesitated. He had always dealt in bonds because they couldn't be checked easily. Stocks were something else. The certificates were registered, so most forgers wouldn't touch them. But the cut was too great. One last big kill, and then I can do what I've always dreamed of.

The idea came to him after he'd talked to the Frenchman. He would leave the world of forgery with a loud bang. He would shake it until its teeth rattled. He would do the impossible. One negotiable certificate for 10,000 shares— one million dollars. One. The idea made him tingle.

Then the whole deal had grown bizarre. First, the unexplained roundtrip ticket to Bordeaux. Then, the faceless meeting in the white room of that weird house with its maze of coils and humming generators. "Your contact is Iris," the voice said. And Mannie, accustomed to identifying faceless voices, knew it was the same man who had ordered the wine labels. "Fifty thousand now. The balance when you deliver the documents."

It took months of steady work to execute the final product. Then the trip to Albuquerque, his surprise to hear the breathless voice of a man when he called "Iris," the fatalistic sensation when he dropped the envelope in the box, and at last the magnificent exhileration of $200,000 delivered to his hotel room. They'd paid off! The nuts had paid off. And he'd gone bounding up to Santa Fe for a wild holiday.

Now the pot of gold at the end of the rainbow had turned to a pot of shit.

He took another drink from the bottle and sat on the

three-legged chair. He leaned back against the wall. It was
cold on his spine. He squinted at the painting. The wizened
face returned his stare.

The bitch!

How had she figured it out? What had he done to give
himself away? The counterfeit bills? That had been small
talk, nothing. How the hell had she zeroed in on him?

The painting.

His work had always been perfect, uniquely perfect. But
his first original creation contained within it his first flaw.
And it had given him away. He had copied so expertly for
so long he couldn't think of, or apply himself to, originality.
He had copied the finest thing he'd ever done. The Greek
goddess on the front of TC stock. Iris.

Well, that had to change. Everything had to change.

If Lexey Jane really knew as much as she said she did
about Mannie Ringer, the dogged old bitch could put him
in prison. She scared him. She had money, power, contacts that could force him to run and hide the rest of his
life.

Bang!

He leaped from the bench. It was only a door closing
somewhere in the neighborhood. But it had the sound of
an iron gate. He froze, half-standing, listening to the night.
His nostrils widened, sniffing for danger. This is what it will
be like, Mannie Ringer. The rest of your life. You'll be fro-
zen like this everytime you hear a match light.

At first, he sidestepped the idea. But with each drink of
the scotch, it grew stronger. Survival roiled inside him,
knotted into a steel ball beneath his ribs. And the twisted,
alcoholic logic strengthened him.

Who would question it? An old, crippled broad dies acci-
dentally. Who would question it? She's lived her life. Mine
has only started. She's the only obstacle.

And then . . . he sighed heavily, then you are free. Forever. No more. This is the last thing.

He emptied the bottle, then phoned the hotel.

"I'm sorry. I just saw Mrs. Pelazoni leaving," the clerk answered.

The receiver slid from his hand as he hung up. His palms were drenched with sweat. Suddenly, he whirled. He grabbed the wet brush from the floor and slashed it across Lexey Jane's face, then ran outside and jumped into the pickup.

It did not dawn on him until much later that it was the first time he had willfully destroyed one of his masterpieces.

Lexey Jane held the sheet of paper beneath the lamplight. A sketch for a tapestry, my foot! It was a map! A map drawn with Peaches' careful lines. She looked at the polyhedron-shaped object in the upper right-hand corner. It was a crystal. All the lines zigzagged toward it, terminating at that spot. She pointed her finger at it. "Dr. Filiamo, if you are in this work, that is where you are."

She grabbed Peaches' billfold and stuck it in her own purse, dressed so hurriedly she slipped her shoes on the wrong feet. "Oh, fiddlesticks!" she cried. She grabbed her cane and, as swiftly as she could, tottered toward the elevator.

She didn't have to go far. She'd seen the sign across the street from the hotel a dozen times. She pushed open the heavy door and smiled hopefully at the small man with a double chin standing behind the desk.

"I want to rent a car."

He peered over his glasses at the wall clock. Nine forty-five. "You just made it," he answered morosely.

"Oh good." she smiled.

He eyed the cane . "Uh . . ."

"Oh, this." Lexey flipped it into the air like a baton. "It's just for looks."

"Oh," he sighed. "Okay. Now if I can see your driver's license."

Lexey Jane pulled Peaches' billfold from her purse and flipped quickly to it.

"I'm not really supposed to be here," the man went on as if he owed himself an apology, "but the regular girl had to leave early, so I came down to close up." He looked at a contract form on the desk. "Let's see. I'll need some identification."

"Just keep the billfold. I won't need it until I get back."

He glanced up at her. "Okay, I'll need your signature here."

She scrawled Peaches' name across the blank.

He took some keys from a hook. "The car's down below in a garage. I'll walk down with you."

"Oh, no. No, that's all right. If you'll just describe it for me, I'll find it."

"Okay." His two chins rolled with weary gratitude. "It's a light blue four-door sedan. Parked near the elevator. Here. This key will unlock it. You sure you know how to drive it?"

"Of course!"

Lexey Jane tottered out as briskly as she could. She talked to her knees: don't give out on me now. This may be the most important exit you will ever make.

Downstairs, she spotted the car and sighed. Thank the Lord, he didn't insist on coming with me. She slid beneath the steering wheel and looked for the gearshift.

"They have put it back on the floor!" She stared indignantly at the stick protruding between the seats. She tried to move it sideways. It would only go back and forth. She chewed her lip. "Let's see. On my 1948 Hudson, it was on

the steering wheel. Surely the principle is the same."
She tried again. "Oh, Henry Ford, they have ruined
you!" she cried in exasperation.

She turned the ignition and stepped on the gas. The tires
screeched as the car lurched backward into a concrete pillar. Her head snapped forward. The sound ricocheted off
the walls. "Oh dear God! I hope no one saw me do that!"

Putting it in drive, she carefully steered it through the
narrow entrance. "Ah." She settled back in the seat. At the
first stoplight, she glanced again at the map beside her. It
seemed to be in the same direction as Jerry and Annie's pyramid. But then it had been daylight. If she could only remember in the dark . . .

She was on the highway. A car coming toward her
blinked it lights. "Oh my." She fumbled for the knob on the
dashboard and her lights blazed on. "That's much better."
She waved an apology.

A car was behind her now. She held the map up in the
beam of light coming through the rear window. Let's see,
the line on Peaches' drawing zigzagged up a mountain,
then a turn to the right.

The car was so close now its lights were blinding her. She
turned the rearview mirror to the side. Suddenly, the
mountain was in front of her. The car began to jerk. It
spurted in quick lunges. Pain sped through her. "Oh!" she
cried in frustration at the gearshift. With all her might, she
shoved it forward, and the car roared up the mountain with
shrill, piercing speed.

The dirt road suddenly appeared on her right. It was on
the map. Gripping the wheel with all her strength, she
turned. Her fingers knotted in agony. Tires screamed. The
car careened back and forth on loose gravel as she hurtled
through the dark.

Indignantly, she glanced at the headlights still behind her. Why was it following her? *Following her!* "Oh, Lexey Jane, you fool!"

To her right was a black hole—a dark cliff plunging straight down. She clutched the steering wheel and pushed her foot down hard, trying to huddle close to the mountainside. But the other car was already there! It was on her left, swerving, twisting toward her, pushing her toward the cliff.

"Ahhhh!" She felt the front wheel slip, fall, then cling to the narrow road. The sharp curves rushed at her out of the dark.

Faster. I've got to go faster. Her hand raked the gearshift. Her foot slammed against the accelerator. The car hurlted into the air. It leaped backward, the wheels locked in reverse. Her shoulders rattled in their sockets as the crash whipped her backward, then threw her against the steering wheel.

From the corner of her eyes, she saw the other car slam into the side of the mountain. It was a pickup! She had whipped into the bed of the truck and slammed it against the mountainside.

Something was wrong. She cocked her head. Quiet. It was quiet. "Oh, my God!" she cried. The engine was dead. "Oh, Henry Ford, don't give out on me now!"

Out of the swirl of dust, she could see someone crawling from the truck. "Start, damn you! Start!" Suddenly, a clattering, grinding racket burst from the engine, and she was moving. The car groaned up the dirt road. She gulped. Her mouth was dry. "Except for that awful noise, it drives quite nicely." She patted the steering wheel.

But her knees were shaking, bobbing up and down uncontrollably, causing the car to spin through the night like a jerking comet. "Now just pretend you're Barney Old-field," she told herself, "and you're on the speedway. It is the last race. It is the race of a lifetime. Oh, don't talk like that!"

A fence sprang in front of her. Too late. The car roared and clanked right through it. Wire flung itself wildly against the windshield with loud cracks. "Oh dear!" she cried. The fence tangled in the bumper and ricocheted back and forth against the hood. The curled wire caught at the tall weeds like a tentacle. Her head snapped back and forth as the car lurched on. Rocks flew up against the underside, pounding her from beneath with deafening bangs.

Through a thick group of trees, a large house loomed up in front of her. Gripping the steering wheel, she braced herself and plunged down on the brake. The car twisted, swerved, and slid with a screaming, grinding halt. She leaned forward to catch her breath. Then slumped back against the seat. "Well, Mrs. Holmes, the invasion of Normandy was a bit more subdued."

The knees will have to go, she told herself. If they don't behave properly, they will have to go. She moved her tongue around her dry mouth. She fumbled for her cane. At some point, it had rolled under the seat. She hadn't the strength to reach it. The knees will simply have to pull themselves together, she ordered.

Pain pulsed through every inch of her. She moved her arms. They still worked. Slowly, she opened the door and climbed from the car, only to be doused in an instant flood of light that that exploded through the trees. She tried to walk toward it. The jagged rocks caught at her feet, throwing her off balance. She clasped one hand over her eyes, just as a hand took her arm. "Here, let me help you." A gentle, soothing voice wrapped around her. She felt herself leaning toward it, allowing her shaking knees and pained body to be braced by this stranger who was smiling down at her as he led her to a doorway. A warning pricked her like a safety pin breaking open. But I've used up all my fear on all the wrong things, she thought regretfully.

"Watch your step now." The voice moved her rhythmically down a short flight of stairs into a room with soft light. Her heart banged against her ribs, but she kept sinking into the strength of this man.

Where had she seen him before? In the bar that first night, of course. But before that? Something so familiar about his face. She looked up at him in a querulous daze. His small eyes were set close to either side of the long, narrow nose. Full nostrils. The mouth a thin line. Where have I seen that spatulate face before? Where?

"I've been waiting for you, Mrs. Pelazoni."

"How did . . . ? Who told you I was looking . . . ?" She couldn't make the words come out.

"My assistant told me of your interest. Jerry Kirwen."

Before she could reply, his hand closed around her arm. She floated through the rooms, down corridors and passageways like a toy boat pushed along by this strange man with the familiar face. The high-pitched sonic whine of machinery swirled around her as they stepped into a room filled with huge generators, dials, exotic switches. Tiny lights winked and flashed at her from the walls. Entrails of tubing ran everywhere, up the stairs, beneath doors, along ceilings.

She put a hand to her ear. The sound was splitting.

"You are hearing nothing more than the sound of a defective toaster or a television set in your living room." Dr. Filiamo smiled kindly at her. "It's not harmful." He stopped to glance around the room. His admiration of it was pas-

sionate. "In the octaves just below the lowest note on a piano are vibrations harmonizing with the alpha, beta, and
theta wave cycles of the brain. I am working on waves even
beyond those." He looked down at her, his face wreathed in
some mystic pleasure.

"I don't understand," she whispered. What's happened to
my voice? It's hollow. It's floating outside of me.

"Come this way," the gentle, rhythmic voice was saying,
and she was following him as if he were some irresistible
magnet.

He led her into still another room, white, antiseptic and
quiet. In the center, beneath a long glass tube hanging
from the ceiling, was a bed. A crib. And asleep in it was
Devon McCarthy.

"Oh, dear God! You've brought the boy here!" she cried.

"So he can be healed," Dr. Filiamo said gravely.

"But his mother! She's frantic . . . they're looking for
him!"

"We'll return him safely. It only takes a few hours." Dr.
Filiamo walked toward the crib and gently touched the
boy's arm. "Fili will make you well," he cooed to the child.
Abruptly, he looked up at Lexey Jane. "Do you know about
the wave spectrum, Mrs. Pelazoni?"

What was he saying? She'd wandered into an old Frank-
enstein movie by mistake. Lexey Jane edged toward the boy
to see if he was all right.

"You see," Dr. Filiamo went on in that quiet, soothing
voice, "at the very top of the spectrum are the unknown
waves of pulsing stars. Further down the scale you find long
radio waves, aircraft control, normal radio broadcasting
frequencies, then there are the FM, television, ultra-
high-frequency waves, and radar. But at the opposite end
of those pulsating stars, far below the infra-red, beyond

x-rays or Gamma waves are . . ." his voice hushed, "the unknown waves inside the nucleus of the atom." He turned to her triumphantly. "That is what I am working on, Mrs. Pelazoni."

"Devon . . ." Her voice was feeble. Something was pulling at her.

She was next to the crib now. The child's breathing was steady and deep. The flushed strain was gone from his face.

Dr. Filiamo was gazing up into the glass tube that hung above the crib. "I have been using a pulsed laser field"—his voice fell suddenly to a flat and businesslike whisper—"of mercury neon emitting a laser beam in the frequency of 9.4 billion cycles per second. This laser was excited by a high-frequency magnetic field, in turn generating an extremely high-frequency beam."

What is he talking about? She could hear his mesmeric voice, but not the words. They swam past her on the electric air. Her body was relaxing. She felt herself nodding at him as if she understood.

"That pulsating laser beam," he went on in a soft whisper, "produces a laser magnetic field two thousand times that of earth. This is very close to Gamma radiation. In other words, Mrs. Pelazoni . . ." He savored the pause. "I am exciting the basic curative abilities of the body itself." He gazed gently at the child. "More than that, after he's cured, he will be immune forever. It is the same with cancer—no recurrence—even broken bones mend within a day's time. And wounds heal beneath the rays in a matter of minutes."

He looked at her beseechingly. "Jerry said you might want to . . ."

"So this is where Peaches Mueller's money went. This machine."

Dr. Filiamo nodded with a strange expectancy. Oh dear God, she thought with panic. Jerry's told him I want to give him money. He thinks that's why I'm here!

"Who killed Peaches, Dr. Filiamo?"

He suddenly exploded into agitation. He let go of her arm and paced the floor. "I don't know. I don't know." He seemed truly grieved over his ignorance.

"But you did know she was murdered, didn't you, Doctor?" A tiny muscle in her eye was warning her.

"Only because there was no way for her to die with the treatments she was taking. I know that."

"Then who gave her the stock certificates?"

He began to mumble. His smooth, undulating movements were gone. He walked in rapid jerks away from the crib. "I don't know. I don't know."

Charades again. "Dr. Filiamo, a man with your scientific knowledge cannot be that stupid!" she snapped at him.

The child stirred in the crib. How could she stand here talking about stocks and bonds? "Dr. Filiamo, the boy. We must call. Is there a phone? His mother is not in too stable a condition as it is, and . . . Dr. Filiamo?"

He stopped in a far corner of the large white room, turned, and flung out his hands. "Mr. Hiatt was in charge of all funding. He hoped to make a fortune once the machine could be patented. There's one being built in France, and he was concerned that I get this one finished first. He sometimes got quite frantic about it."

"He was found dead, Dr. Filiamo. How did he die? Do you know?" She heard her voice high and thin in the room. I must get out of here. Somehow, I must get Devon and me out of here.

From across the room, Dr. Filiamo twisted and looked helplessly distraught. He glanced this way and that.

Maybe he really doesn't know, she thought. Maybe all those things they say about scientists are true—that they bury themselves so deeply in their work they don't even know when they've got an abscessed tooth. Maybe Hiatt did just hand him the money. Maybe he didn't even do that. Hiatt could have bought the equipment for Filiamo.

She tried once more, whispering over the head of the sleeping child. "You knew the certificate was a forgery, didn't you?"

He shook his head sadly. His face lifted and he looked at her so beseechingly and with such anguish that she felt his torment. Poor man. Just wanted to invent something to cure the world. And look where it's got him. We'll get the boy back to the hospital. I will call Julien. No sense being persnickety right now . . . not with a boy's life in danger. Besides, Mannie is the key. Julien would be furious if he slipped through their fingers.

"Dr. Filiamo, please, I must call the hospital. I must let his mother know where he is."

He took a few uncertain steps toward a door. "He's safer here. He will be well in the morning. Better than all those tubes sticking in him . . ." He was mumbling, grumbling, as Lexey Jane tried to follow him.

Her toe caught in a coil roped across the floor. "Even this appears a bit cumbersome, Dr. Filiamo." She almost shrieked with pain, trying to catch her balance.

"Ah yes," he sighed, dismayed. "But I have received a recent instruction for a simpler method. A much simpler method."

Lexey Jane's foot stopped on the stairs. A dread prickled her. "An instruction?"

"Yes." He smiled at her with that familiar flattened face. "You see, I am a reincarnated Atlantean."

"A what?"

"Atlantean," he explained, "from the lost continent of Atlantis. There are many of us—reborn in anticipation of the Aquarian Age. I receive my instructions while in a trancelike state."

Lexey Jane's eyes closed, slowly, painfully. I am not here, she told herself. I really am not here. I am in the Elgin Theater on Eighth Avenue watching an old horror film. In a moment, if I open my eyes very slowly, in a moment I will smell popcorn from the lobby.

But a strong hand was gripping her arm, pulling her back across the room toward a door on the far side. Dr. Filiamo ceremoniously flung it open. "You really should see it, Mrs. Pelazoni," he commanded, shoving her into a darkened room.

She sucked in her breath. Hollow eyes blinked at her. Transparent teeth grinned cadaverously. The room swelled with a blue aura as brilliant lights shot from the death face. The crystal skull. In the center of the room, it rested on a table covered with a black cloth. It leered at her as the halo of blue light swirled around its crystal brain.

"You stole this!"

"It was necessary that I obtain it. For experimental purposes."

The gentle, rhythmic voice was gone. His tone was so formidable, she jerked toward him. He had closed the door and stood inside the light radiating from the skull.

Lexey Jane stepped closer. Along the cranium, a galaxy of tiny air bubbles winked at her like stars. Like dazzling memories trapped forever.

"Why?" she whispered. She could not take her eyes from its macabre beauty. It was a sculptured jewel with dreams dancing inside.

"I will stimulate this crystal skull with an electromagnetic coil. It will then maintain a consistent vibration of waves for infinity. You see, the shape of the skull has the perfect combination of axes. That, combined with the crystal structure, will give off cosmic energy—the one universal energy. The very same energy the alchemists searched for. It's here, Mrs. Pelazoni. Inside this skull."

She wasn't listening to him. The skull held her. It was like a glimpse into the silent center of the universe, into all the memories of the human soul. Into complete knowledge and wisdom. A transparent promise of all the good and beautiful things. I know where they are, Rebecca West; she remembered the letter still stuck in the bottom of her purse. All the good and beautiful things have slipped away into this.

The magnetic pull was so powerful, she felt her pulse slowing. Her heart was scarcely beating. She was floating toward it, floating on the rainbow aura. This is how Iris must have felt, flying with wings along the spectrum on an errand for Jupiter.

She could hear music. A soft, faint remembrance of melodies weaving in and out of whispers. A thousand whispering voices. A chorus of blessing. She tried to pull back from it.

Catch onto a thought, Lexey Jane.

But the magnetic pull was too strong. Her brain felt rearranged, soaring, splitting, shattering into a million stars. The skull was sucking her into it, calling to her with its crystal sirens.

"I will be implicated, won't I?"

Startled, she looked at Dr. Filiamo. Had he spoken? He would not stay still. He was all blue and kept swaying back and fourth. No. It was she who was swaying.

Talk to your knees. Hold together, knees.

"The counterfeit stock. Will I be charged?" He was still looking at her.

Where have I seen that face? The odd spatula shape, the long nose with full nostrils, the small eyes—where?

"I'm afraid there will be some . . . an investigation of some sort." The words were wrenched from her in tiny gasps. She didn't want to speak. She wanted to look at the crystal skull. She wanted to feel its glassy mind with her fingers.

Now what is he doing? Why is Dr. Filiamo groping around on the floor in the dark? Ah, there he is. Where have I seen that face before? He looks so strange in the blue light.

What is that he's holding in his hand? Sparks are shooting from the end. Little crackling sounds. It's making the hair on my arms stand up, the fillings in my teeth throb. It is a coil. An insulated coil. Only the end of it is alive. He is going to electrocute me.

"Dr. Filiamo!" She tugged at the strength somewhere inside her. "This is nonsense!"

"No. I have worked twelve years on this machine. Twelve years of my life . . ."

A deal. A deal? How do you make a deal with a madman? Someone who thinks he's from Atlantis. She flung out her arms.

The skull.

She clasped it to her, wrapped herself around it. It was cold. She could feel the iciness against her breasts. "I will drop it, Dr. Filiamo," she threatened. "I will drop it, and it will shatter into a million pieces."

"She's bluffing."

Mannie Ringer towered in the doorway. He closed it behind him. "I know her too well. She's in love with the past. She won't drop it." He sneered at her.

"Don't be so sure," she whispered.

He moved toward her. A trickle of blood had run into the creases on his forehead. It was Mannie in the pickup. It was Mannie she'd run into the mountainside. What was it Holmes did to Moriarty? He threatened his status, his reputation, that frailty of the ego. You've threatened to destroy a human dream, Lexey Jane. And there is no more time for games. This is real. Mannie Ringer is real. And he is going to kill you. They are both going to kill you.

She moved back. I will move slowly back into the dark, make my way around to the door. But the blue aura from the skull radiated around her, lit her up like neon.

"Don't!" Dr. Filiamo was screaming at Mannie, rushing at him with that sparkling coil. "It the perfect one! The others are copies! This is the only one!"

"I don't give a shit about your crystal skull!"

Mannie hopped back and forth, dodging the snake Dr. Filiamo kept poking at him. "Goddamn you!" he screamed. "Can't you see she's got us both? Help me, you bastard!"

"She'll drop the crystal!" Dr. Filiamo whined.

Now where is Mannie? He's disappeared. Ah, there he is. On the floor, sprawled on the floor with Dr. Filiamo. She could hear dull thuds, hear them grunting as they rolled over and over. The coil. The coil was flicking across the floor. Leaping and twisting.

Dance. Dance around the room. Waltz, Lexey Jane. The Nazis are after you. Waltz. An American can outwaltz a German any day. Reverse. Dizzy. Giddy. Wet. Dripping wet. A jagged pain up her right leg. Doesn't matter. Keep waltzing. The music is still playing.

The coil whipped along the floor, hit the table leg, bounced back. Suddenly a hand reached out of the blue light. Her head snapped forward. She sank her teeth into the wrist. Waltz, Lexey Jane. Dance over there. Now reverse. Twirl. Your hands are wet. Slipping. Dry one. Then the other. Hold on.

"She won't drop it, goddamn it! You're in this as much as I am!" Mannie was shouting again as he sprawled full length across the floor. Dr. Filiamo was on top of him, his arms wrapped around Mannie's legs. The coil had caught beneath the table leg and lay there spluttering.

"No, No!" Dr. Filiamo was heaving, pummeling Mannie with his fists.

Now Mannie is on top. He has Dr. Filiamo by the throat. Waltz with your back to the wall. Around and around the room. Don't stop. Wars have been won and lost with waltzes.

She could hear the steady beat of a drum. One, two, three. One, two, three. But it is not a drum, Lexey Jane. It is Dr. Filiamo's head pounding against the floor. And he is not moving any longer. And Mannie is panting like a huge beast.

He is slipping money to the orchestra leader so the music won't stop. I know he is. No orchestra can play this long without a bribe. Strange, you can even hear the thin shriek of silk dresses around you. No, Lexey Jane. Mannie just pulled the cloth off that table. He's coming toward you. He looks like a bullfighter. Manolete. Is there a dance like that? Never mind. Don't think. Waltz. Be nimble, be quick.

Mannie's arms were around her. He was crushing her. The skull. It was slipping. It would shatter like stardust. Silently.

The cloth was over her head, pressing tight against her face. She gagged. He was stuffing it in her mouth, into her nose. Mannie was right. She never could have dropped that crystal. Terrible for someone to know your weakness.

She felt the hardness of it somewhere in the folds of cloth wrapped around her. Her ribs crunched against it. The Mummy. The Mummy is back, ladies and gentlemen! We dare you to stay seated to the end.

Where is the popcorn? Where?

An exhausting, excruciating fatigue washed over her. Her mouth throbbed. Each bone in her body was snapping. One by one.

I sound like kindling. Now I'm floating, drifting . . . not yet! Not yet, Lexey Jane! You are Ruby Keeler and you must make your heart tap dance. Don't let it stop. Dance.

She could hear a child crying. The high, piercing whine of machinery grew louder and louder. It shrieked in her ears. The drums had started again. No. They were footsteps. A voice was shouting.

"We know you're in there, Mrs. Peltzioni! You've done it this time!"

And Bennie Montoya was standing in the doorway, still finishing the sentence as he pulled his gun.

There was a crack. Mannie screamed and grabbed his shoulder. Bennie's paunchy sidekick lunged into the room with his holster swinging and knocked Mannie to the floor.

Lexey Jane felt Bennie's strong hands untangle her from the black cloth. "You all right, Mrs. Peltzioni?" Someone was groaning. She braced herself on Bennie's arm and looked around a room of exhausted faces, ghoulish in the eerie light. Dr. Filiamo's hand had melted around the coil. His body jerked on the floor as the current coursed back and forth through him.

"It's stopped," she gasped. "The orchestra finally stopped." You're wrong, she corrected herself. There's still one more dance.

Chapter Nine

"You're more trouble than a busload of wetbacks."

Lexey Jane noticed *his* knees were shaking as he drove her back to town. There had been those tense, sad, juxtaposed moments while they waited for the Sanchez Funeral Home to pick up Dr. Filiamo and a patrol car for Mannie, during which Bennie had exhibited a courage even he didn't know he possessed. Then the ambulance with Shiela flying from it in her cloak, like the good witch of the west, enveloping a very sleepy, confused Devon in its folds.

Now Lexey Jane and Bennie rode in silence for awhile, trying to control their knees as the real horror of the night seeped through them both.

"I got a call from that friend of yours in New York, and he said to put you on the next plane if I had to rope and hog-tie you."

"Julien said that?"

211

"Not exactly those words. Then I got a call from the fella who runs that Avis place."

"I'm lucky he knew I was using a dead woman's driver's license."

Bennie chuckled. "I think what concerned him most was you backing into that concrete pillar."

"Now I really did quite well, considering I haven't driven in eighteen years."

"Jesus!" Bennie laughed.

"How did you find me?"

"I was at the hospital seeing about that kid jerked outa his room when I got the call from your friend. That Shiela said you'd gone to find Dr. Filiamo."

"You knew him?"

"Most complaints we get are about that nut blowing all the fuses with that equipment he's got up there."

"I'm always asking the wrong people the wrong questions." Lexey Jane shook her head.

"I want to thank you." She laid a hand on his arm as he pulled up to the hotel. "Thank you for saving my life."

Bennie stumbled around for words. "I . . . it was . . ."

"And you may have to do it again."

"What are you—?"

"Please. Please don't ask me any questions. Because the answers I'd have to give would really convince you I was crazy."

Bennie looked at the old lady as he parked the car in front of the La Fonda. Here was this octogenarian, crippled, at the end of the line, and with more spunk than he'd ever encountered. His own mother was content to make tortillas and kneel in church five times a week. He had to admit he was beginning to like her. And if she had something else up her sleeve, he was willing to go along. It was more exciting than going home to an empty house and a can of beer.

Lexey Jane opened the door to her room. "Would you mind waiting in the bathroom, Captain Montoya? I expect a visitor and I need you here."

Bennie whistled through his teeth. "Jesus, this is going to be a real, honest-to-god Agatha Christie night!"

Lexey Jane flashed a smile at him. "You . . . ah . . . you will have some company in there shortly. But please don't say a word. Trust me."

Bennie nodded.

"Oh, Mr. Montoya, is there anything you'd like while you're waiting? A drink perhaps?"

"Sure. I'll have a Tacate beer."

Lexey Jane frowned. "I've never heard of it."

"The bartender will know."

"Of course. I'll have them send it right up to you."

She closed the door and quickly made two phone calls.

In a moment, the beer was delivered. Lexey Jane tottered to the bathroom with the tray and knocked on the door.

Bennie opened it and peered out. "I feel like a fool." He resumed his perch on the toilet seat.

"Well, don't. You've already been a credit to your profession once tonight, and they say opportunity always knocks twice. Here. This will help pass the time."

She handed him the beer with the salt and lime, and watched curiously while he smeared the top with the juice, salted it down, and took a deep, grateful gulp. "You know," she sighed, "I've never cared for beer, but that looks quite delicious."

"Would you like to try it?" He handed the can to her.

"No. No, thank you. Later."

She closed the door behind her, and took a sip of the

warm gin she'd ordered for herself. She turned off all the lights but one dim bedside lamp. Then she sat in the chair facing the door to wait. The knob turned; Lexey Jane stiffened. A friendly face. She pointed to the bathroom and leaned back in the chair. Through the wall, she could hear whispers between her guests. Not some ghost-blurred chant in a pyramid. Real whispers of real people. My world, she smiled to herself. At that moment, the knob turned again.

"Hello, Jerry."

He leaned against the door, locking it behind him. "Really ought to keep this thing locked." He grinned at her, then padded across the room in his sneakers and sprawled on her bed.

Lexey Jane frowned at the insolent possession of her room.

"Watcha been up to?" His eyes gleamed at her.

"I've been hunting crystals up in the mountains."

"Oh, that's dangerous."

"I think it may be more dangerous right here."

His eyes widened in mock surprise. "You're a nosey old lady, you know that?"

"You mean the little ruse with the flying saucer trick didn't quite get me acclimated?"

"Pyramid didn't get you either?" He chuckled revoltingly.

She gripped the arms of the chair. "No."

"Too bad. It's all scientifically proven."

"That's good. I'm glad you believe in it, Jerry."

"I kinda thought you were different. But you know something? You're like all the rest of them."

She watched the young face twist into an ugly snarl.

"You mean if you can't get money from me, I'm no good to you," she answered sadly.

He gave a tiny, spastic shrug. "You're all alike. You're all rot. You pollute the world with your money. You suck the world dry with it."

"Oh, Jerry," she whispered. Would he understand the rebellious youth who boycotted the cotillion ball? Was there a bond between them? No. This is different. This is ugly, sick, dreadful. "You murdered Peaches, didn't you?" she asked softly.

"As my contribution to ecology."

"And wired my bathroom . . . ?"

He grinned grotesquely.

" . . . and Mr. Hiatt?"

He suddenly looked crestfallen. "I wanted to put him in the pyramid . . . see if he would mummify."

Lexey Jane blanched. "But how . . . ?"

He began to say the name. She could hear the sound from his tongue. "Don't. Don't tell me." She shook her head, shuddering. *I don't want to hear it. To think he trained the dog to kill . . .*

His face kept contorting into a strange smile. "Oh, yes, we must protect the delicate feelings of little old ladies who own factories and build pipelines and destroy the world so they can eat more steaks and get their feet massaged and have all their expensive operations . . . " the nonsense spewed from him.

"You killed them all? Why? Why?"

"You're all the same. The more you shrivel up, the tighter you clutch that money. The more you destroy. You are the evil in this world."

Not once had he raised his voice. It rolled around the

room in a hollow monotone. "Look what you've done. Look how you've messed up the world. You take everything that's alive, and you dig your heel in and grind until you kill it. And all to make more money."

She knew then. No logic. No logic in the universe would work with this one. She sat listening while all the ache of the sick world coiled in the room.

"You know what Mrs. Mueller did with her money? She played little games with it. Little games to make people squirm." He gave that short, empty laugh again. "But I got it out of her. I learned how to play games, too. Hiatt and I found something to dangle in front of her. Her own vengeance. Clever, don't you think? An old family feud over one of your big corporations." He giggled. His pale hair fanned out from the static electricity in the room. "We shoved her own shit right back down her throat."

"Hiatt was a distant cousin. He knew Peaches' one great weakness, set up a plan with you, then . . . then why did you kill him" she asked thinly.

"He was no longer of use." Jerry's face bristled with venom. "The bastard threatened to mess up the whole deal with his spy games."

She saw the pitted face lying on the table, the face desperately hanging onto youth. Poor Rudy Hiatt, jogging and darting about in his tennis shoes, replaying antique spy roles. "He got the counterfeiter for you," she sighed wearily, "with the help of the Frenchman."

Jerry's head twisted at her. His mouth slid into a maniacal grin. "You bitch. You mean you know about that? Too bad . . . too bad that goddamned greaser caught you falling out of the truck." He shrugged. "Could have saved all this trouble. You see, Lexey Jane, *we* save the world. We don't spend it."

With that languid motion of his body she had so admired, Jerry took the pillow off the bed.

So this is how you fix pollution. You snuff it out.

Her hand shot forward. "The money. Where is the money?"

"Poor old lady. You mean you don't know where the money is?" he sniggered. "Knows everything but where the money is. Isn't that a shame. You'd like to know that, wouldn't you? Money. The most important thing to you. Goddamn!"

He moved rapidly at her. His eyes glittered like glass. The air closed in. He was crouching over her. The suffocating silence of the pillow was inches from her face.

"She's not dead."

He stopped. "Who?"

"Peaches. Mrs. Mueller. She's not dead. You believe in the unified field theory, don't you?" The words were coming too fast with fear. She struggled to make her voice steady and firm.

He squinted at her, frowning. She could smell his breath.

" . . . the equation for bringing atoms and molecules back together again, into their original form." She was talking rapidly now. The pillow was so close she could feel the gagging choke in her lungs. "Well, Dr. Filiamo did it. He brought Peaches back."

His face slackened, then abruptly twisted into a sneer once more. "You stinking liar."

She put out her hand. The pillow was on her face. "No, Jerry! I mean it!" Her shout was muffled. "Listen!"

From the darkness of her bathroom, a voice spoke. It bounced off the tile and floated into the room with a hoarse, monstrous whisper.

"Jerry."

His mouth half-opened. He was so close to her, she could see the twitch begin at the corner of his lips.

"Jerrrrry," the voice moaned again. A dress rustled. The smooth young face leaning over her grew rapt. She heard him laugh under his breath.

Then again, the whispered, haunting murmur, "Jerrrr-ry."

Stealthily, he backed away, a nauseous smile on his mouth. The pillow dropped to the floor. He reached behind him and turned the lock.

Bennie Montoya bolted from the bathroom and crashed against the body half-jammed in the door. They tumbled into the hall. She heard a howl of rage as he shackled Jerry's arms behind him.

Lexey Jane heaved a sigh and leaned back in the chair. "It worked," she whispered incredulously to herself.

At that same moment, raucous male laughter roared from her bathroom. "That was a helluva lot more fun than the late night movie!" A head of cropped white hair peered around the door.

"Thank you, Miss Boydon."

Chapter Ten

Julien Strauss left his office early. He had an important appointment before going to the airport. The taxi dropped him at an office building on Broad Street. He made his way through the smell of fresh latex paint and worn marble to the top floor. Down halls, across a mammoth room sprouting desks, computers and secretaries, until he reached an executive-looking reception room. Beyond another door, Kathryn Wyler looked up from behind an immense desk.

"Julien!" She greeted him with an edge of caution to her brightness.

"I'm taking you to lunch."

"Oh, Julien," she teased. "You're supposed to take black people home for dinner."

He ignored her. "We have a celebration to attend." He raised his hand. "Long live the TC empire."

Kathryn braced herself against the desk. "You found the counterfeiter."

"Without alarming the SEC, notifying the CIA, exciting the FCC, calling in the FBI, employing the Secret Service, or—" he bowed slightly— "crumbling Wall Street. Yes. I have found the counterfeiter."

"Oh, Julien!" Kathryn Wyler ran from behind the desk and flung her arms around his neck.

"On second thought." He smiled. "It might not be such a bad idea to take you home for dinner."

At La Guardia, Julien checked his watch and hurried toward Gate 3. He squinted at the figure walking toward him in the distance. He took off his glasses. Put them on again. It couldn't be. Then she waved. Julien gasped.

Gone was the elegant meerschaum-headed cane. In its place, a serpent twined up a stick of olive wood, and firmly attached to its head with unblinking turquoise eyes was Lexey Jane, dressed in a faded blue denim skirt and western jacket with silver studs. "What in the . . . ?"

"You should be grateful I'm not in jeans." She laughed. "Even I thought they were a bit much. But I had to have a souvenir of Santa Fe." She turned slightly, leaning on her new cane in a stylish pose. "It's the best brand you can buy," she reassured him. "And the label was so appropriate, I couldn't resist it. It's called 'Faded Glory.'"

Julien was still chuckling as he helped her into the taxi. He puffed down on the seat beside her and took her hand. "I'm glad you're back. Safely."

Lexey Jane glanced up at the eyes that looked so blue-green in the sun. Maybe that's it, she thought. Maybe it's his eyes that tantalize all the young women so.

She squeezed his hand. "Oh Julien, there's such a *sameness* about you. It's so comforting." At that moment, the taxi swerved to miss a car. The driver shook his fist and shouted out the window.

"And such a reality about New York," he laughed.

She reached for her purse that had fallen on the floor and saw the letter from Rebecca West still in the side pocket. She crumbled it and tossed it out the window.

"What was that?"

"A memory that needs to be thrown away. Not everything stays the same," she sighed.

Maybe Julien would like Shiela. They were both such worriers. Shiela reminding her at the Albuquerque airport to "call the moment she got to New York." They had both stood in the bright sun laughing like teenagers, calling each other "Watson" and "Holmes." It had been gratifying to see the strained, ashen look gone from Shiela's face. Devon was well on his way to recovery, and she was even beginning a new book. "I'm not going to worry about you," Lexey Jane had said, laughing, "you're cut on the bias."

"And what does that mean?" Shiela had asked.

"It means no matter how many different ways you're stretched, you're going to hold together."

"You've got that funny look on your face again," Julien said.

She jumped at the sound of his voice pulling her back. "Oh." She tossed her head. "I was just wondering if you'd be interested in Frank Parcher." Suddenly, she looked wistful and glum. "Julien, how is Mannie Ringer doing?"

"His work is so good, that even he is having trouble telling which certificates are the real ones." Julien lapsed into silence, then puffed an unusually contrite sigh. "You know that yours could have been counterfeit instead of Mrs. Mueller's."

Lexey Jane turned to him slowly, her eyes rounded in mock surprise. "Why, Julien. The idea simply never occurred to me."

"You're lying, and you know it."

Lexey Jane pursed her lips. "I never could have considered it; otherwise I wouldn't have been able to take the train to Santa Fe." She gazed out the window. "I hope the court is not too severe with Mannie."

"Lexey Jane! He tried to murder you!"

"That's because he was desperate."

Julien rolled his eyes to the ceiling of the taxi. "That is why most murders are committed," he answered flatly.

"Julien, where is the money?"

"Gone."

"All of it? A million dollars?"

"You cut anything five ways, and it goes fast."

"Jerry, Mr. Hiatt, Mannie, the Frenchman . . ."

"And Filiamo. As far as I can tell, he spent his on that machine. Captain Montoya found about two hundred thousand in Mannie Ringer's suitcase. Can't find Hiatt's cut yet. Duplessis will be more difficult. He's already slipped by on one scandal. And that young hoodlum has lapsed into some kind of catatonia."

"But Annie Mueller will get what's found?"

"Yes," he assured her. "It will take time, but according to the last—and I mean the last time Mrs. Mueller revised it—will and testament, Annie will get it."

"And the crystal skull?"

"Arrived safely this morning and it will be returned to Mitchell-Hedges' daughter immediately."

"Oh dear!"

"What's wrong now?"

She wrung her hands. "I feel as if I may have set medical science back two thousand years."

"Don't worry. It's alive and well in Bordeaux."

Suddenly, she sat forward. "Julien! I know where I've seen that face before! Dr. Filiamo's." She turned to him in great excitement. "On Easter Island! Those great stone faces planted on Easter Island."

But Julien was shaking his head violently, "No, Lexey Jane. No, no, no, no, no . . ."